# Death and Peaches

Sugar Creek Mystery Series

Book Two

Nova Walsh

Two Worlds Press

Published by Two Worlds Press, LLC

Cover art by DLR Cover Designs

www.dlrcoverdesigns.com



Published in the United States of America.

First Edition, 2024

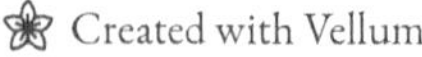

# Chapter One

T*he stars at night, are big and bright...Deep in the heart of Texas.*

The song had bounced around my head ever since I'd crossed the border from New Mexico to Texas nearly two days before. As I spotted that first "Don't Mess with Texas" roadsign, the melody intensified in my mind. It was a song that most of us Texans learned in the cradle. Certainly I had.

I'd arrived back in the Texas hill country that afternoon after a very long drive from Los Angeles, my little Honda packed to within an inch of its life with all my worldly possessions. It was the height of summer, nearly July, and instead of the beautiful wildflowers I'd enjoyed when I'd visited in April, the hills were now brown with dead grass and shrub. It was not the ideal time to be moving back to Texas in terms of the weather, but it suited me fine otherwise. Back in April, when I'd visited Sugar Creek to help my Aunt Meg cater a wedding at her B&B, I'd made a plan to move back as soon as my L.A. apartment lease was up. Aunt Meg needed help to get more business, and the plan was to turn her B&B, Primrose House, into an event destination on top of the overnight guest business she currently ran. I was itchy to stop working for other people after culinary school and to start a catering business of my own, so the idea of helping her out with events had turned out to be a perfect fit for the both of us.

Just like when I visited in April, I got a little teary as I pulled off the highway into my hometown of Sugar Creek. The pickup trucks lining Main Street, the statue of a longhorn in the square that kids in town loved to climb, and the sprays of lavender and salvia all around really brought me back to my Texas roots. I'd been gone too long.

But there was nothing that could compare to pulling up in front of my best friend's shop to really pull me into the Texas state of mind. Her antique shop, Divine Finds, was all things Texas, and my heart pitter-pattered with excitement as I parked at the curb outside. I hopped out of the car and stretched a while, so tired of driving that I silently vowed not to sit for the rest of the day. As I walked up the steps, I grinned wide, knowing that I was only seconds away from seeing my best friend Cassie Divine in person once again.

I pushed through the door just as she was coming out of it and we collided and laughed, falling into each other's arms.

"Lady!" Cassie's voice rang out like the sweetest melody, full of warmth and years of shared memories. "Welcome home! Gosh, I missed you!"

I gave her one more squeeze, then followed her inside the shop. The comforting scents of cinnamon and vanilla met me and I instantly felt the weight of the road lift. "I missed you too. It sure is good to be home."

"I bet. I thought you'd be here earlier."

"The traffic through El Paso was no joke. I would have gotten here a lot sooner, but there was a major accident that held everything up."

A few customers meandered through the antique shop,

looking at the wares Cassie had collected from countless estate and yard sales over the past year of being in business. She walked back behind the counter and sat on a stool near the cash register, motioning to an overstuffed velvet armchair across from her.

So much for vowing not to sit. But the chair was delightfully soft as I sat and I kicked off my sandals, snuggled into the corner, and tucked my feet under me.

"Well, you're here now! I don't know what you had planned for the night, but I was thinking we could go over to Lulu's for dinner after a while."

I nodded. "That sounds great. First, I want to unpack a little and I was thinking about heading over to Primrose House to visit Aunt Meg for a bit. Maybe we could do that on the way to dinner, if you don't mind?"

"Of course!"

We caught up, Cassie telling me about adventures in antiquing and I telling her the details of the very long drive I'd just finished. We were deep in conversation when two women approached to pay for their purchases. They were in the middle of a lively discussion, their voices tinged with disbelief, as Cassie stood to ring them up.

"I still can't believe it," the first woman said, shaking her head as she placed a vintage teapot on the counter. "A fistfight, right there in the council chambers!"

Her companion, clutching a set of embroidered napkins, chimed in. "I know, right? I thought those council meetings were about as dull as a mashed-potato sandwich, but today was like something out of a TV drama. Councilman Landers and Councilman Weiss, going at it! They're way too old to act that way, if you ask me. They should be ashamed of themselves, grown men acting like teenagers."

Cassie wrapped the teapot carefully in paper and chimed in. "A fistfight? That's crazy! What over?"

The first woman shrugged as she handed over her credit card. "Something about that bill they're trying to pass. It's caused quite the stir. I wish everybody would just simmer down. The heat is going to their heads."

"Yeah, more than likely," her friend added, "although I've heard that bill might change the whole landscape of Sugar Creek, especially for small businesses. So it makes sense they're riled, I suppose."

"I know the bill you're talking about. Seems like everyone in town is up in arms. You're right, if it passes, it'll be mighty hard to keep the big franchises from moving in and changing things," Cassie said.

The women nodded as they pulled out their wallets to pay.

One of them leaned into Cassie. "I heard Councilman Weiss is being bribed by one of those big lobbyists from Austin." She glanced around the shop quickly. "Don't say you heard it from me, though."

Cassie handed the women their purchases, her brow furrowed. "I hope it's just a rumor. He sure has a lot of power around here. But I guess that would make sense why there's so much fighting. Time'll tell, right?"

The women nodded and smiled.

"Thanks for coming in, ladies. Take care now," Cassie told them with a wave and a smile before sitting back down with me.

As the women left, I turned to Cassie, my curiosity piqued. "What was that about? A bill changing the landscape for small businesses?"

Cassie sighed, leaning back against the counter. "Yeah, there's been talk around town. This new bill, if passed, could open the doors for big franchises to come in. It's a real threat to mom and pop places in town. That's why things are getting heated. Some council members are all for it, thinking it'll bring growth. Most, though, are worried it'll hurt the charm and character of Sugar Creek."

I felt a twinge of concern, thinking about my own plans to start a small catering business. "Sounds serious. I should probably look into it before I go apply for my business license."

Cassie gave a small, reassuring smile. "Don't worry *too* much. This town's always been about supporting its own. Even if the bill gets passed, I don't think it'll be as bad as some folks are making it out to be. But it sure has people's tails up."

Before I could say another thing, the chime sounded from the front of the shop. "Yoo hoo!" A call floated back to us and Cassie jumped up. I would know that voice anywhere, and I jumped up too.

Aunt Meg and her employee Maria, who I'd become close with in April, made their way back behind the counter, all smiles.

I grinned, my heart melting, when I saw the woman who'd practically raised me. I squealed and gave them both big hugs. "You didn't have to come over. I was planning on visiting the B&B in a bit."

Aunt Meg waved a hand. "It's no problem, honey. I know you've been in that car for days. And I just couldn't wait." She squealed and squeezed my hand, and I smiled. "Our girl is back for good!"

Cassie pulled two more chairs over and we all sat and caught up for a few minutes. Aunt Meg told a story about a toilet leak that had us all laughing, and Maria told us about her daughter preparing for a trip to Dallas with a school group.

After a while, I leaned in to Aunt Meg. "I have a few ideas for the B&B I want to run by you. I had a lot of time to think on the drive," I said with a laugh.

"I can't wait to hear them! We need all the help we can get. But you must be dead-dog tired. Why don't you stop by in the morning and we can let our imaginations run wild."

I nodded. It was true. The drive had taken a lot out of me. But I was buzzing with creative energy and excitement to get my business off the ground. "Okay. It'll have to be early though. I have a lot on my plate since the Peach Festival is the day after tomorrow."

Maria lit up at that. "Oh, I've heard so much about the festival. I plan to take Daniela. Will you be cooking for it?"

"Yep. I signed up as soon as I knew I'd be coming back for sure. The Peachy Keen contest is what I'm angling for. It's the biggest cooking competition in Sugar Creek. Best peach related entry wins. The Peachy Keen title goes pretty far in this town, so I thought it would be a good brag for my new catering business. And I can hand out samples and business cards to people at the festival. Hopefully, I can get some business flowing right away."

I turned back to Aunt Meg. "Tomorrow I have to do most of the cooking for the festival, but I also need to stop by town hall and file my paperwork for a business license. It's all filled out. I just need to go turn it in. I also need to stop by Wild Hare in the morning. Mark and Sheila said I could use their van for the festival, so I can drop by the B&B before I go pick it up."

Mark and Sheila Connoly had been our neighbors since I was a child. They owned Wild Hare Winery, a beautiful artisan winery near Primrose House that had grown considerably with the influx of tourists over the last decade or so.

"That'll be fine. I should be around until noon at least. I've got a Zumba class at one though, so make sure to come before then." It wasn't a surprise. Aunt Meg was in her late sixties, but she had more spunk and energy than most teenagers I knew.

After a few more minutes, Aunt Meg stood, and Maria followed suit. "We won't keep you girls. We just wanted to drop by and say hi, and we've got to get back to the B&B to set up for happy hour. Hope y'all have a good night. And don't stay up all night long gabbing like you did when you were girls. Y'all need your rest!"

Cassie and I laughed, knowing that in all likelihood we would do exactly that—stay up all night gabbing.

"I'll come by in the morning and we can talk business," I told

Aunt Meg, and she grabbed me for another hug, nearly squeezing the daylights out of me.

"Get some rest. I'll see you in the morning!"

Cassie followed them to the door, flipping the closed sign and locking it behind them. "Okay! I know it's a little early, but I declare that business hours are over. Time to have ourselves some fun!"

# Chapter Two

After I'd brought my things in from the car and gotten settled into Cassie's cottage that sat directly behind the antique shop, we decided to walk to Lulu's, which was only a few blocks down from Divine Finds on Main Street. It was hot out, but the sun was on its way down, so it wasn't totally unbearable. I loved strolling down the street, reacquainting myself with all the shops and restaurants that made up the business district of Sugar Creek. Being home made me want to leap for joy after the hectic bustle of L.A.

"How are things going with Ty?" I asked as we strolled. She had been dating deputy Ty Clayburn when I'd been back for the wedding in April, and from what I'd heard from her over the phone, Ty had forgiven her for her role in our questionable sleuthing during that time almost immediately, their romance resuming like nothing had happened.

Cassie smiled and tucked a strand of hair behind her ear as we walked. "Pretty good. He's been dropping a lot of hints lately about marriage. I don't know though, we've barely been together a year."

"For some, that's more than enough time to make things official. Seems like you two are pretty close to perfect, from the outside at least."

She sighed, a smile on her lips. "He is an amazing man. Supportive, quiet, respectful. I do very much like him. I'm just not sure I'm ready to make that big decision yet, you know what I mean?"

I nodded. I'd barely had any long-term relationships myself, and since I was still decidedly single at thirty-two, I didn't have much insight to add.

We arrived at Lulu's to find a few people waiting in line outside. The warm glow of the neon sign flickered like a beacon in the dusky Texas evening. The familiar scent of smoked brisket wafted through the air, mingling with the sounds of laughter and country music that spilled out every time the door swung open. We leaned against the wall and continued to talk until it was our turn to go inside and order. At long last, after the smoke had done its magic and made me hungry as a bear, we finally entered the restaurant.

Stepping inside, a cozy chaos enveloped us. The restaurant was bustling with energy, a symphony of clinking glasses, sizzling grills, and the hearty chatter of locals enjoying their meals. The walls, covered with vintage Texas memorabilia and old black-and-white photos of Sugar Creek, radiated a rustic charm that put me in a nostalgic mood.

As we approached the front counter, the mouthwatering aroma of barbecue intensified. The man behind the counter wore a checkered apron smeared with the day's work and greeted us with a jovial, "What'll it be tonight, ladies?"

We ordered quickly—ribs and coleslaw and a sweet tea for Cassie, and sliced brisket, baked beans, and Lulu's special sweet potato casserole with a Dr. Pepper for me.

With our orders placed, we finally slid into a booth near the back and leaned in to hear each other as we waited for our food.

"I still can't believe you're back for good! Sugar Creek hasn't been the same without you. And now, you're actually going to live with me! It's like our high school sleepovers all over again, but with wine!" She said.

I laughed. Aunt Meg had offered me a room at the B&B but I'd decided to bunk with Cassie instead because I didn't want to take up a room that Aunt Meg might otherwise rent out. And Cassie had been so giddy at the idea of the two of us living together that I couldn't say no to her invitation.

"Like I told you before, though. I'm only staying on one condition! You have to let me do most, if not all, of the cooking while I'm here."

Cassie grinned and sipped her tea. "Well, if that isn't the deal of the century, I don't know what is."

We leaned back and watched the bustle of the restaurant for a few minutes. I was overjoyed to be done with the move from L.A. finally. It had weighed on me for months, and all the work of wrapping things up in California and figuring out what would come next had drained my energy. Not to mention that drive. Boy, it was good that it was finished.

"I wonder how serious that stuff about the council bill is," I asked, twirling my soda can slowly around before taking a sip. "That sounds like it could mean trouble for me if it goes through. I'll have to do a little digging tomorrow. See if I can find out anything about it on the internet."

Cassie nodded. "I know a lot of folks have been up in arms. It doesn't really affect me or my antiquing business as much as the food and beverage places in town, but I can understand the opposition. It wouldn't be good if the character of the town changed and I think that's what would happen if a bunch of franchises and big box stores start to come in."

We were interrupted by our food arriving. Lulu herself brought out two trays and set them in front of us.

"Abby! Hey girl! Your Aunt told me you'd be comin' back to town. Good to see ya! I don't have time to talk now, but stop by sometime during off hours and we can talk. I heard you're starting a new business, gonna give my little B-B-Q place some competition. Good on ya!"

Lulu's barbecue had been an institution in town for more than twenty years and I knew that me starting a catering gig would be cutting into her business, so I was surprised she was so friendly about it all.

"Okay, will do. Thank you, this looks amazing!" She gave us a quick wink and a grin, then headed back to the kitchen.

I tucked into the delicious dinner, the sweetness of the casserole balancing perfectly with the salty tang of the smoked meat. They had great food in Los Angeles. Food that people paid an arm and a leg for. But there was nothing quite like Texas barbecue.

A few minutes into our meal, Cassie leaned in, eyes twinkling with mischief. "Ryan has asked about you nearly every day since I told him you were coming back. You should see him, Abby. He's like a teenager. Blushing, agitated. I think the sheriff has a crush on you."

I blushed myself, the heat rising to my cheeks, and sipped my drink, trying to hide my growing smile. "Really?" I asked, my voice barely above a murmur. "I've been missing him too. I was hoping something might happen between us now that I'm back in town, but I didn't want to get my hopes up too much. It's been a while since we last saw each other. Hopefully, he's forgiven me for the... incidents around Trisha and Greg."

A few months prior, I'd catered a wedding at Aunt Meg's B&B when one of the bride-to-be's enemies turned up dead. Cassie and I had done a bit more snooping than we should have, and had ended up in hot water with Sheriff Ryan Iverson and Cassie's boyfriend, Deputy Ty. But along the way, the sheriff and I had grown feelings for each other as well. At least *I* had grown feelings for *him*. I wasn't too clear about his feelings. We'd emailed back and forth some over the last months, but mostly it was getting-to-know-you kind of things, not what I would call romantic in any way, so I wasn't sure if the interest ran both ways.

Cassie's expression softened with understanding. "Oh, Abby, everyone makes mistakes. And if I know Ryan, which I think I do, he's been counting the days until you came back."

Suddenly, Cassie's face lit up with an idea. "I've got it! What if we do a double date? You and Ryan, Ty and me! It'll be fun, casual. No pressure."

My heart harrumphed at the thought. "A double date? I don't know, Cassie. It's been so long since we've seen each other. A date might not..."

Cassie reached across the table and grabbed my hand. "Oh, honey. No. He is ready to date you, and you are ready to date him." She smiled a sly, knowing smile. "I can see it all over your face."

I let out a small, nervous laugh, the idea growing on me quickly. The thought of seeing Ryan again, but with the security blanket of Cassie's presence, was suddenly very appealing. "Okay, fine. A double date. But let's keep it low-key, okay?"

Cassie clapped her hands in excitement, her energy infectious. "Absolutely! Low-key is my middle name."

I raised an eyebrow, and she giggled, then shrugged. "Well, I can try."

"Okay. But not until after the Peachy Keen competition. And it better be casual, Cass. I don't want it to feel like a romantic date. Just a friendly catch up." I wasn't sure about it, but I also didn't want to keep going down this line of thinking. Best to agree with her and shove all thoughts of Sheriff Ryan Iverson out of my mind for the time being. I had a business to start, after all, and a competition to try to win. I needed my wits about me.

Her grin made me nervous. It was sly and calculating and I could tell she was hatching plans that I probably wouldn't like. Matchmaking plans.

I focused on my dinner and eventually steered the conversation in other directions. After a while, I finished every scrap on my plate and licked the fork clean, leaning back in the booth with a satisfied smile. “You’re going to have to wheel me out of here.”

Cassie laughed and patted her stomach. “I know, right? It should be a sin to make people want to eat too much. Alright, you ready? I have a bottle of wine at home with our names on it. I bet you want to get to bed early, too.”

I smiled and nodded. The drive had been exhausting. And I had a full day tomorrow getting ready for the festival. But I was ready to work, and excited to be home.

# Chapter Three

Waking up the next morning, I was immediately buzzing with energy. I was so excited to get things going for my business that although I still felt sore and tired from the drive the day before, I couldn't stay under the sheets any longer. The morning sun filtered through the curtains, casting a gentle, warm glow across Cassie's spare bedroom, where I would be staying until I got myself off my feet. I stretched, feeling a sense of purpose and excitement for the day ahead. It was my first full day back in Sugar Creek, and I already had a laundry list of things to do to get my catering business up and running.

The smell of freshly brewed coffee beckoned to me from the kitchen, a comforting reminder of the simple pleasures of home. Cassie was already up, humming to herself as she poured two steaming cups of coffee.

"Morning, Abby! Did you sleep okay?" she asked, sliding a cup across the counter towards me.

I sat on a barstool and took a grateful sip, the rich flavor revving me up even more. "I slept great. That bed is divine." I laughed at my joke and she laughed too.

"I've got to go over to Fredericksburg this morning. There are a couple of estate sales I need to hit up. Stock for the shop is getting low. But I should be back sometime this afternoon. Here, let me give you keys for the shop and house so you can come and go as you please. I made them myself."

I almost spit out my coffee, and she burst out laughing. When I'd been here in April, we'd gotten into a barrel full of hot water after she'd copied a set of keys Ty was in possession of with the key machine she had in her shop.

"Glad to hear you're using the key copying machine for good purposes," I replied, taking the keys and slipping them into the pocket of my jeans.

"I've got a busy day, too. Lots of work for the festival tomorrow. I'll probably be over at Primrose House most of the day prepping for the festival."

Cassie nodded. "If you need to cook here, you're welcome to!"

"Thanks, I might just do that, actually. It'll be easier than going back and forth from Primrose House. I won't do it for the catering business. I need to work out of a commercial kitchen, and that's what Aunt Meg's B&B is zoned for. But for the festival, when I'm just handing out samples and taking part in the competition, it shouldn't be a problem. And, if you're around, maybe you can be my taste-tester and give me some feedback! I'm still not sure what I'm going to turn in for the competition tomorrow. I have three options, and I'll do samples of each. But I want to have it figured out before then so I can make sure to have my best work on the competition entry."

"I love it! I'll be a taste-tester any day. I should be home before dark."

We enjoyed our coffee together a few minutes longer and then went our separate ways. I had so much to do before I was ready for the festival and not much time. I grabbed my notebook, filled a travel mug with another cup of coffee, and hit the road.

The drive to Primrose House was short but scenic, the familiar streets of Sugar Creek passing by in a blur of quaint storefronts, kids playing in the park, and tourists meandering. It wouldn't be long before the summer sun chased everyone inside, but the morning was still pleasant enough to coax people out. My mind raced with potential recipes and ideas for the festival and for my business as I made my way to the other side of town where the B&B was.

Aunt Meg and I had agreed that I would use the B&B kitchen for all of my catering activities, at least until I could afford to do something different. I still had debt from culinary school, so I wasn't starting out with much. It would give me a major advantage to not have the expense of renting a kitchen right off the bat.

I pulled into the Primrose House parking lot and hopped out of the car with my coffee. It was heating up quickly, but I didn't rush as I made my way up the stone path to the wide front porch. Even in the heat of the summer, Aunt Meg managed to have lovely flowers blooming in beds surrounding the porch. Bees buzzed in the lavender and the eponymous primrose that snaked a pink path along the edges of the walk.

Stepping inside, I found Maria at the small podium they used as a check-in desk near the front of the sitting room, and I smiled. "Good morning! It's so quiet in here."

"Hello, Abby! A tour bus just left with a group of guests, but it's a little slow right now too. Although we have several reservations for the weekend. People coming in for the Peach Festival, I believe."

I frowned and nodded. I was sure our annual festival would attract quite the crowd of tourists. But it worried me that business was slow. Ever since Aunt Meg had confided in me about her money woes in April, I'd been worried about her and the B&B.

"Do you know where Aunt Meg is?"

"Last I saw, she was out back working in the flowers."

"Thanks!" I told her and headed down the hall that led to the kitchen and the back door. The kitchen was old, but it was cozy. To the right there was an ancient refrigerator and a walk-in pantry.

A large wood block island sat in the center of the kitchen and a window over the sink looked out to the backyard. Near the far wall there was a kitchen table and a sideboard where Aunt Meg had coffee, tea, and snacks set out for guests.

Instead of heading out the back door to find Aunt Meg, I took a few minutes to reacquaint myself with the kitchen. The space would be an important part of my business. Although I'd grown up in this very kitchen, it had been a long time since I'd regularly used it. After our parents died in a car crash when I was eight, my brother Devon and I moved into the house with Aunt Meg and our Uncle Nolan. This was the kitchen where my love of cooking had been born. It was where I learned to make sugar cookies for Christmas and Thanksgiving turkey with all the trimmings for the big get-togethers my aunt and uncle had held for all the neighbors every year.

This kitchen was where my dreams of being a cook had been born. So it was fitting that I was starting my business here in this same kitchen.

Before I could reminisce any further, the back door opened and Aunt Meg came in, knocking her tennis shoes on the concrete step before stepping onto the kitchen tile. "There you are! I saw your car in the lot."

I smiled and gave her a quick hug. "Just looking around a little, thinking about what needs to be done to get this old kitchen up to snuff."

"I wish it was a better setup. But we'll make it work, right? If it was good enough for Marlene's wedding, it'll be good enough for anything else you might cook up." She laughed.

"That's true. I might want to buy a portable fridge before too long. That was certainly a problem for us the last time around. But yes, things should be fine for a while at least. And if I grow big enough, we can always think about an addition, or I can find a place in town."

She waved that thought away. "We'll figure it out. Now, let's hear those ideas you've got. Because, as you can probably tell, our guests are drying up and we need to get some more business coming through here pronto."

We moved to the kitchen table and Aunt Meg grabbed a cup of coffee before she sat down. I pulled out my notebook and turned to the first of many pages of notes I'd made over the last couple of months.

"Thanks to Marlene's event, we know we can get a solid wedding business in," I began. "You said you've had a few calls for weddings for next year already?"

Aunt Meg nodded. "I wasn't sure what your plans were then, so I didn't commit, but now that you're here and ready, we can reach out and see if they're still interested."

"Ideally, for the B&B, it would be good to do events that would bring people in from out of town so we can get the guests staying here too. Business events could be good as well. We did a lot of business events at the place I worked in L.A. Corporate retreats, that kind of thing."

"I like that! I could talk to Shirley at the chamber of commerce, see if she can think of some ideas to spread the word."

"The other thing I was thinking about was maybe doing a fancy dinner now and then. We could charge a hefty price and make it really exclusive. I could split the earnings with you as a sort of space rental fee, because the beauty of this place is just as important a part of the magic as the food would be. I know there are a couple of tour companies that set things up for groups and we could see if they'd be interested in recommending it to their people."

"I saw something on Pinterest that might work for that." She pulled her glasses on and opened her phone. After scrolling a moment, she handed it over to me and I smiled. It was a picture of a beautiful evening garden party with twinkle lights and country decor.

"That's perfect! Exactly what I had in mind. The B&B guests

can take part or not if they want. It's up to them. And locals or tourists staying elsewhere can come and hopefully fall in love with our space and spread the word. We could start with one and see how it goes, but eventually I was thinking it could be a somewhat regular event. We might even want to get one going in the next week or two, just to get the word out."

Aunt Meg sat back and grinned, then sipped her coffee. "I love this. It is a fantastic idea. The weekend after next would be good. So far, we have nothing planned, but there are a few reservations for rooms. I can reach out and tell them about it, see if they want to attend. We can keep it fairly small at first, and charge a little more. Make it seem more exclusive that way. Which it will be. We could even make it seasonal. I have so many ideas for seasonal decorations and we already have quite a stash of decor for the B&B we could make use of."

I opened my notebook immediately and started scribbling notes. I was so totally engrossed in my planning passion that I forgot where I was for a moment before Aunt Meg's laugh interrupted me.

"Here I thought I might be putting you out by convincing you to come back home, but it looks like you're right in your element with this idea and this business. It's so good to see you doing what you love. And so good to have you back here so I can watch you do it in person!"

I closed the notebook and grinned. "You're right, I do love it. I've never had so much fun. I just hope running a business doesn't prove to be too difficult. There are so many things to take care of! Speaking of which, I'd better get going," I said as I looked at the clock on the oven. "I need to get over to Town Hall and register for a business license."

Aunt Meg drained her cup and stood, nodding. "Good luck, honey. I'm sure it'll be a piece of cake."

If only she'd been right.

# Chapter Four

Ten minutes later, I pulled up to the curb in front of the town hall, an old brick building that stood like a relic of times past amidst the modern bustle of daily life. It had a faded red brick façade and the steps leading up to the large wooden doors were worn smooth from generations of townspeople coming and going.

With a mixture of nerves and excitement, I gathered my paperwork and stepped out into the heat, feeling a wave of hot air greet me. I sighed as I pulled the old oak door open and stepped inside a cool interior that smelled faintly of polished wood and history.

Blessed air conditioning.

I walked through an open lobby and found a sign of office locations and then made my way down the hall to the public records office. Pulling the door open, I found a small tidy lobby with a few worn leather chairs against one wall and historical photos of Sugar Creek lining the other. I approached the reception desk, my heart pounding with the anticipation of officially starting my new venture.

Thankfully, there wasn't a line. Although this being Sugar Creek, I suppose a line would have been a surprise. Still, I was so used to the constant throng of people in L.A. that it felt like luck was on my side as I walked straight up to the counter.

I was greeted by a friendly young woman in a ruffled shirt and business slacks. "Good morning. How can I help you?"

"Hi, I'm here to submit my application for a business license," I said, offering her my brightest smile along with my completed paperwork.

She smiled and glanced over my application. "Oh, the caterer! I heard about you! Your aunt was at bingo the other night, telling everybody how you were coming to town to work with her."

Word sure got around. "Yep, that's me."

"Deep in the Heart Catering. I love the name. How fun!" she said as she double checked every line. "It looks good. I'll need to run a few things through the computer and have a supervisor approve it. Give me a few minutes."

I smiled and nodded, trying not to pace, but strolling back and forth in front of the counter, nonetheless. This felt like a very big step in my life. I'd always had inclinations toward owning my own business. I'd sold countless cookies, bracelets, and dolls as a girl. But this felt real. Something about the official nature of the paperwork cemented in my mind the fact that I was about to take on a huge responsibility. I hoped I was up to the task.

Before I got too far in my thoughts, a little man came out of the back room with my papers in hand, the young clerk following behind him with a frown on her face.

The man had a noticeable paunch and a balding head. His glasses sat perched on the bridge of his nose, and there was a perpetual frown etched into his features. But what really stood out to me was a nasty purple bruise covering one eye. I couldn't help but wince as I looked at him.

"I'm sorry, Ma'am," he drawled as he pulled up to the counter in front of me and flipped through my paperwork with disinterest. "But this address is already registered as a business. I cannot approve your request at this time."

I frowned, my excitement quickly turning to frustration. "I know, it's my aunt Meg's B&B. I plan to run the catering business there because most of what I'll be catering are events at the B&B."

He looked down at me over his glasses, his expression unyielding. "That may be the case, but you'll need to have a separate address for this new venture. The rules demand it."

The clerk cleared her throat behind him. "Excuse me, Mr. Weiss. But I thought there was a clause in title six about..."

"That's enough, Gina," he snarled at her, swiveling his head from me to her. "I know you think you're all high and mighty because you went to college, but I still have the final say in which licenses are rejected. We discussed this already. This office will not be used to support rinky-dink businesses that will drag the town down. People who share business addresses are not the kind of people we want in Sugar Creek. Next thing you know, the place will be crawling with food trucks." He rolled his eyes and Gina frowned behind him.

My heart sank, both at the rejection and at his words. How dare he call Deep in the Heart Catering rinky-dink? I may not have started catering yet, but he didn't know anything about my business. Frowning as he handed my paperwork back to me, I could have sworn there was a smug lift of his lips as he did it. This man got off on power. It was clear as day.

"I am ready to take clients. I have my food permit. I have a certificate from a culinary institute. My business is going to be a shining pillar of this community once it gets off the ground." I could hear my voice rise, but it couldn't be helped. I was just getting started. "My aunt's kitchen has been approved as a commercial kitchen because of the B&B. This is absurd," I argued, my voice rising with each word.

He said nothing, only stared down his glasses at me.

Frustrated, I growled and shook my papers at him. "This is ridiculous, sir! You should be ashamed of yourself!"

I turned on my heel in a huff and immediately realized several other people had entered the small lobby while I'd been on my tirade and were blatantly staring at me as I performed my monologue. I pasted a smile on my face, hoping no one here was a potential customer. "Howdy, y'all," I said quietly as I straightened the papers in my hands and adjusted the purse on my shoulder, deciding suddenly to lean into the drama. If nothing else, drama would get the town gossip wheels turning. It might just help me spread the word about my business, so why not embrace it?

"Y'all think this is exciting, you should try my cooking! Deep in the Heart Catering. I'll be in business whether this clown approves my papers or not! You can bet your butts," I said as I shook my rejected papers in the air. Although I regretted it as soon as I'd said it. Mr. Weiss was clearly not amused as he scowled at me, making the shiner on his face look even more awful. I flinched, despite myself.

Probably didn't make him any more likely to approve my license in the future, but I was not in the mood for being reasonable.

There was nothing left for me to do. Not this day, at least. So I smiled my best smile at everyone, said, "have a nice day," and then quietly made my way out of the permit office and through the cavernous empty lobby. As I stepped back into the heat of the day, the door of the town hall closing behind me with a definitive thud, I sighed. Despite Aunt Meg's wishes, that had *not* been a piece of cake. That hadn't gone well at all.

# Chapter Five

When I got back to Cassie's place, the first thing I did was pull out my laptop to research this new bill I'd been hearing about. I remembered that one of the council members the women had been talking about the day before had been named Weiss. And because of the shiner on his face, I would bet anything that the man who'd rejected my license had been the same Mr. Weiss that had been in a fistfight at the council meeting. The rejection of my license was fishy to me, and I couldn't help but wonder if it had to do with the bill that the women had been talking about. I couldn't imagine him rejecting me because of that, but I had to be sure of what I was dealing with.

Luckily, the internet had plenty of information for me, both for and against the bill. Various interest groups had their hot take and after half an hour I felt like I understood what was going on, at least as much as could be gleaned from research. Who knew the truth about what was going on behind the scenes?

As I delved deeper into my research, it became clear that the bill in question was a contentious piece of legislation related to franchise laws within Sugar Creek. At its core, the bill proposed a significant shift in the local tax structure, one that would heavily favor large franchise operations over small, independent businesses. By offering substantial tax breaks and incentives to franchises, it would effectively tilt the playing field away from local entrepreneurs. The more I read, the more apparent it became that this bill would not only open the floodgates for big chains to enter Sugar Creek but also potentially suffocate the charm and uniqueness of our small town with an onslaught of generic, corporate entities.

This revelation struck a chord in me. It wasn't just about my struggle to get a business license; this was a larger battle for the soul of Sugar Creek. The online debates raged fiercely, with local business owners rallying against what they saw as a threat to their livelihoods, while proponents of the bill touted the potential for economic growth and job creation. And there, in the center of this storm, was Councilman Weiss, a staunch advocate for the bill.

I found a campaign picture of Mr. Weiss, confirming that the angry little man was indeed now Councilman Weiss. He'd been voted into office just recently, although he'd been in charge of the permit office for over a decade, and I wondered who in their right mind would support such a mean person for public office. I had no doubt he'd pulled the wool over the eyes of the people of Sugar Creek. I didn't know if it was my anger at his ill-spirited rejection or pure curiosity, but part of me wondered if he had come by the appointment through purely ethical means. It wouldn't surprise me to learn the man had been into something shady. The comment from Cassie's customer popped into my head, the one about Weiss potentially being bribed by a lobbyist. I wondered who else might know about this little detail, and just how legal it all was.

Before I had time to research any further, though, Cassie came through the cottage door with a huge box and I jumped up to help her inside.

"Find some good stuff today?" I asked her.

She laughed and nodded as she set the box on the kitchen table. "Too much, unfortunately. The shopping part of my business is certainly the funnest. But gosh, it's going to get me into trouble if I'm not careful." She pulled a set of delicate gloves and a beautiful antique table lamp out of the box. "How 'bout you? How was your day?"

I sighed and leaned against the kitchen counter, crossing my arms over my chest. "Not the best."

She set her wares aside and frowned at me. "What happened?"

I told her about having my business license rejected, and anger for me flushed in her face.

"Can you believe the nerve of that man?" I huffed as I paced the room. "Who ever heard of such a ridiculous rule? Clearly, he is just being spiteful."

Cassie nodded and headed for the fridge. She grabbed a bottle of white wine and poured us each a glass. I took mine with gusto and drank the first sip a little too fast, nearly choking on it as I did.

"You wouldn't be the first to have problems with Weiss. I've heard all sorts of stories about run-ins with him. I think Georgie had trouble when she first wanted to open Henderson's Fine Foods. You should talk to her, see if she has any insight on how to get the license through. There might be a way around him. I mean, he's not the only one who works at the licensing office."

"But as he so helpfully pointed out to that poor woman who worked for him, he 'has the final say in which licenses are rejected'. I don't know that I have any hope here." I felt desperate and a little scared. It was horribly uncomfortable. I had to get moving or I would combust, so I went into the kitchen and pulled an apron on over my head.

"You could probably get a license over in Blanco or Fredericksburg. Although you'd have to have a business address there. But I bet you could just do a PO Box and call it good."

It was a last resort, but a decent one. "I'll think about it. For now, I'm just going to have to do the festival without the license. They can't stop me from giving out cards and samples."

"That's the spirit. You go, girl. Don't worry, Abby, you'll get over this and it'll just be something for us to laugh about in a year's time," Cassie said with a smile. I smiled back. She was so good at lifting my spirits, no matter how low I was. What would I do without her?

"Okay, here's my plan for the night," I said, ready to change the subject as we sipped our wine and she sorted through her box of goods. "I have to do a lot of the prep work for the festival tomorrow. But I was thinking, if you want to hang out with me, I'll feed you as I go. And you can tell me all about Ty or the antiquing business..."

"Or Ryan," she interrupted with a sly smile.

I blushed and moved to the fridge to pull out a log of goat cheese I'd stored there earlier in the day. "Or Ryan," I agreed.

"Sounds like a plan. And maybe when you're done, we can watch an old movie."

I grinned. "I love it." Pulling a puff pastry out of the freezer and unboxing it, I unfolded the frozen sheet on the cutting board. I'd learned to make puff pastry from scratch in culinary school, but after several experiments, I'd come to the conclusion that the frozen stuff was just as good and took a heck of a lot less work.

"What are you making for the competition tomorrow?"

"I haven't decided for sure, but I was thinking about testing a couple of things out on you and we can decide together which one wins. The first is a goat cheese and peach tart with prosciutto and thyme, the second is grilled chicken and peach skewers, and the third is a peach crumble cheesecake."

She grinned at me. "I knew having you move in with me would be awesome."

I grinned back, so happy to be where I was. In L.A., I'd had two roommates who I never saw and were as busy as I was. This connection was something totally different, and I absolutely cherished it. "I made the cheesecake earlier. It takes a while to set up, so I needed to get it done early. I figured that even if I don't use it as my entry for the Peachy Keen competition, I can hand out lots of samples. I'm sure they'll go fast."

Cassie's eyes grew wide as I pulled the cheesecake from the fridge. "It needs the peach topping still, but otherwise, it's done."

"Holy moley, Abby! I'm going to have to get a gym membership with you here."

"I'll work on the tart now so I can see if I need to adjust anything. I came up with the idea on the ride out here, but I haven't actually tried the recipe out yet. So I'm wary of entering it for the contest before I know how it actually tastes. And we can try the skewers out, too."

I grabbed a bowl of fresh peaches I'd picked up from Tranquil Valley Farm earlier in the day. They were just perfectly ripe with a little give and juices ran out as I began to slice. I worked my way through slicing a dozen of them as we talked, knowing I'd need plenty for the recipes I was testing and for the prep work I'd ended up doing for the festival, then cubed a few more for the skewers. Next, I cut chicken thighs into chunks and marinaded them in a mixture of olive oil, peach juice, fresh garlic and herbs.

"I talked to Aunt Meg this morning. We're going to try out a new idea over at Primrose, a special dinner. It might be monthly or quarterly, depending on interest. But I think it'll be fun. One of my big problems, though, is that I want it to be really classy, very high end so we can charge more. And I know Aunt Meg doesn't have a ton of supplies as far as feeding people. I was thinking maybe you could help me get my hands on some pretty vintage dishes and cutlery without paying an arm and a leg."

Cassie brightened and nodded. I sliced the tart I pulled from the oven, drizzled honey over the top of both slices and brought them to the counter where she sat.

"Yes! I can take you to a few estate sales. I'm sure we can find something. And if that doesn't work, we could always hit up some thrift stores. You never know what you'll find there."

We tucked into the food, demolishing half the tart between us and a few skewers as well. After all our tasting, the tart won out, so I planned to make and serve that for the Peachy Keen competition in the morning.

Sitting back once we finished eating, I sipped my wine, exhausted by the array of dishes between us and the work ahead of me. "So, what do you think? Is the tart good enough to win?"

Cassie looked at the remnants of our dinner and raised her eyebrows. "Honestly, Abby, if you don't win with any of these, I'll eat my hat."

I laughed, the stress of the day melting away in the warmth of the kitchen and Cassie's unwavering support. "Thanks, Cass."

She stood and cleared our dishes, waving me away as I tried to help. "You fed me, lady! Besides, I know you'll have a pile of work to do tomorrow morning. Save your strength for that. I want you to win, and to snag a few dozen customers while you're at it. Deep in the Heart Catering is going to be the greatest culinary adventure that Sugar Creek has ever seen!"

I laughed and blushed. "I don't know about all that. But I do want to be successful. I can't believe that man called my business rinky-dink."

"Why is it that some people have to hate on everything they come across? What a sad way to live a life! Don't you listen to what he said. He's just a little angry man."

"Isn't that the truth?" I said as I sipped the last of my wine. I knew what she said was true, but the words still stung. Despite my culinary skills and my determination to make it work, in my lower moments, I was often terrified that this whole thing was a silly idea and that I was doomed to fail. Mr. Weiss made all those fears and anxieties hover over me like a thundercloud about to burst.

"Thanks for doing the dishes, Cass. I should probably get to bed. I've got to be up at the crack of dawn. I'll try hard not to wake you."

"Don't worry about it, I'm planning to get an early start on the shop. I have to process all this stuff I bought and I want to open early because of the festival. Have a good night. And don't worry, your food is so fantastic, there's no way you won't win."

I gave her a hug and a smile before heading back to my guest room. I sure hoped she was right.

# Chapter Six

I was up the next morning before the sun, ready to slice peaches and roll pastry. My plan was to do most of the cooking at Cassie's before heading over, but I would grill the chicken on a small butane grill at my booth during the festival. With any luck, the smell of grilling meat would attract a crowd. After putting the first two tarts into the oven, I topped the second cheesecake I'd made the day before and cut it into bite-sized cubes, putting each one on a small disposable plate and then onto a tray I would wrap in plastic wrap when it was full.

Two hours of prep work flew by as I baked four tarts, cut all the cheesecake, made the sauce for the skewers, and cut the rest of the chicken to get it marinading. I had an hour left to pack everything up and make my way downtown. Deciding that a quick shower would do me good, I headed into the bathroom, hoping the hot water would help ease the tension in my shoulders. I wasn't nervous about my cooking, exactly. But this was a big day for my business, and the pressure was definitely building.

After I showered, I put on a little makeup and pulled my hair into a pretty bun, then debated between a flowery sundress and cowboy boots or a more sensible slacks and t-shirt. The sundress won, partly because it made me feel special, but also partly because I knew pants would make standing in the heat of the summer unbearable.

A little over an hour later, the early morning sun was already promising another scorching Texas day as I pulled up to Central Park in the center of town, where the Peach Festival would be held. I glanced at my cooling bags and supplies in the back of the van, hoping I could get set up quickly because of the heat. A fine layer of dew still clung to the grass as I stepped into the park, giving the air a fresh, earthy scent that mingled with the sweet aroma of peaches from vendors and booths all around. I made my way to the registration table, where an older woman with a name badge greeted me with a warm smile.

"Morning, dear! You must be Abilene Hirsch," she said as I stopped in front of her.

I cocked my eyebrow, and she laughed. "I knew everybody else who's got a booth, so it isn't hard to guess."

"You got me pegged, that's for sure. Yes, I'm Abby Hirsch. Nice to meet you."

"I'm Mabel, part of the festival committee. Let me show you to your booth." She stood and motioned for me to follow her. "I know your Aunt Meg well. We both attend events at the senior center occasionally. She told me all about you coming back home to start a business. I'm so happy to hear it. Our little town could use some new options!"

As we walked through the rows of stalls already bustling with activity, my stomach flip-flopped with excitement. The festival was a kaleidoscope of colors and sounds—vendors setting up, laughter and chatter, and the ever-present scent of peaches in the air.

Mabel led me to a cozy spot near the center of the festival grounds. "Here you are, dear. You've got a great location—lots of foot traffic."

"Thank you, Mabel. This is perfect," I said, surveying the area.

It was ideal, with enough space for my setup and a nice view of the stage where local bands were scheduled to play later in the day.

As Mabel left with a cheerful wave, I got my bearings. The heat was already making its presence known, causing beads of sweat to form on my forehead. I readjusted my hair, tucking a few loose strands, then made my way back to the Connolys' van to start unloading my samples and equipment.

I had two large coolers full of ice and food that I wheeled over first, trying not to hit too many bumps, hoping my samples would all stay prettily presented on their little plates. The less cooking and prep work I had to do at the booth, the better. I wanted to save my time and focus for talking to potential customers, not fiddling with garnishes and plating.

Next, I brought over a box of tools. Tongs, napkins, plastic forks, extra squirt bottles and toothpicks. I hoped I'd remembered everything. One of the hardest parts about doing this job alone was that I couldn't send anyone off to run errands for me if I forgot things, so I had to get it all right from the very beginning. Luckily, I was an over-planner, and I'd spent hours going through the lists in my notebook, so I was fairly confident I would be okay.

My booth was simple but inviting. I unrolled a banner I'd had printed and shipped to Cassie's house and hung it from the front. It said, "Deep in the Heart Catering" and had a picture of my logo, what I thought was a cute design with a chef hat surrounded by stars inside a circle. I hoped the design and the slogan—"fine food with hill country flair"—would capture the essence of my business for customers. I set out a holder with business cards and a flyer I'd made with a couple of sample menus.

Just as I set my food out on the table, I heard a yip behind me and turned to find a scruffy little dog sitting at attention behind me, his head cocked.

I raised my eyebrow at him and put my hands on my hips, looking around to see if an owner was nearby. "Hey, buddy. How's it going?"

He yipped at me again and wagged his tail, but stayed sitting at attention. He looked just like the dog from the old movie Benji. Scraggly in the cutest way.

"Where's your human?" I asked him. Moving over, I held out my hand, which he sniffed and then gave a quick lick. I laughed and pet his head. It was a lot silkier than I'd expected from his appearance. Looking around, I didn't see anyone nearby. He didn't have a collar on either, which seemed strange. Perhaps he was a stray.

"Go on, now, go back home." I told him and waved a hand. He yipped at me again, did a few quick turns in the grass, and plopped down for a nap. Huh.

"I guess that's fine," I told him and turned back to my booth. He didn't seem to be bothering anyone, and as long as he left my food alone, he wasn't bothering me either.

I arranged my samples meticulously in three rows and started the butane grill. I stretched my neck and shook out my hands when I felt the nerves begin. This was more than just a competition for me. It was a chance to introduce myself and my business to Sugar Creek.

After a few minutes, I stepped back to admire my work, wiping a hand across my brow. The festival was coming to life around me—neighboring booths boasted everything from peach preserves and salsas to handcrafted jewelry and local art. I noticed the man in the booth next to mine arranging an array of vibrant hot sauce bottles on stands. He caught my eye and approached with an easy smile.

"Good morning! I'm Brandon. Looks like we're neighbors for the day. And by the smell of things, I'm in for a treat," he said, nodding towards my peach tarts.

"Hi, Brandon. I'm Abby. Thanks, I hope they'll be a hit," I replied, returning his smile. "Help yourself, if you'd like." I waved my hand at the samples and he grinned, grabbing one of the chicken skewers I'd just pulled off the grill.

"Wow, this is delicious! You know what? I bet it would go really well with my 'Peach Blaze' sauce." He motioned to his booth and grinned.

"Oh really? I love a good sauce. Tell me more!"

"I have a line of hot sauces inspired by a trip I took to the Caribbean last year. I couldn't stop thinking about the food down there, craving it. And I thought putting a Texas spin on those sauces would be fun. So I started playing around, got a little obsessed." Here he stopped to chuckle, and I smiled. I knew all about getting obsessed with food.

He shrugged. "Hot sauce is kinda my thing. In my mind, it's much more than a condiment. It's an experience!" This guy seemed like my kind of person. I followed him over to his booth and picked up one of the pretty bottles on display.

"That's great! Do you mind if I buy a bottle from you? I'll see if I can work it into a recipe or two for some of my events. Heck, if you wanted, we could probably do some sort of cross-promoting. You spread the word about my catering business and I'll talk to clients about your sauces."

His eyes lit up at the suggestion. "That would be so amazing, Abby!" He reached for a bottle on the shelf behind him. "Here you go, the Peach Blaze, no charge. Let me know if you come up with anything. I'd love it if we could find a way to collaborate." He also handed me a business card, which I tucked into the pocket of my apron.

"Thanks, Brandon! I'm sure your sauces will fly off the shelf. And I'll definitely be playing around with this in the kitchen," I said, holding up the bottle. "Good luck today."

"You too," he said with a smile. "Thanks for the sample. It was delicious!"

I turned back to my booth with a smile on my face... and stopped dead in my tracks when I found Sheriff Ryan Iverson standing at my booth, watching me with a dimpled smile.

# Chapter Seven

As soon as I saw him standing there, I was happy I'd chosen the sundress. My face grew hot as I watched him slowly stroll toward me and I patted my hair down, hoping it hadn't frizzed up too much with the heat and humidity. For months I'd wondered whether the feelings I'd started to have for the sheriff back in April were real or not. Over time, Sugar Creek and Ryan Iverson had grown so far away that I'd almost convinced myself I wasn't really as interested as I'd thought. But now that I saw him in person again, my heart galloped away in my ears and I felt every bit as pulled to him as I'd been before, if not more now that I knew I'd be staying in town for good.

We'd shared one kiss back in April and a whole lot of tense moments, but now it was like we were starting all over again. He was just as ruggedly handsome as I remembered, his dark hair curling over his ears, and those blue eyes sparkling as he smiled at me. He cut a good figure in his sheriff's uniform and cowboy hat.

"Abby, hey. It's good to see you again," he said as I made my way back to my booth. I awkwardly moved in to hug him. He leaned down and gave me a side hug, but it was enough to make me all flustered. Yep, I still liked him.

"Good to see you, too." I tried to act cool, but my nerves were all in a jumble. Cassie's boyfriend Ty came up behind us and I gave him a friendly hug, too. "Here, let me feed you two." When in doubt, feed someone. It always worked for me.

Ryan laughed. "I was excited to hear you'd have a booth here today. I remember how good your cooking is. Among other things."

I blushed and waved my hand over the samples, wanting to change the focus. I gave them the low-down on what I had on offer. "Y'all are welcome to try one of each or whatever sounds interesting." Ryan chose the tart first, and Ty took a piece of the cheesecake.

I watched their faces as they ate, lighting up when I saw how much they enjoyed the food. "So good," Ty complemented me. "I could eat about a dozen of those."

"Come back in a couple of hours and I'll let you have whatever I have left."

He laughed. "Sounds like a plan."

"Thank you, Abby. We need to make the rounds, but it's good to see you. Let's catch up later, alright?" Ryan said with a dimpled smile. Boy. He was a looker.

I nodded and watched them walk off. I'd been unsure about where I'd wanted things to go with the sheriff after I'd left in April, but now that I saw him again, I was glad that Cassie had taken it upon herself to set up a double date and play matchmaker. Because now that he was in front of me again, I realized that I definitely wanted to date the sheriff. I only hoped he wanted to date me, too.

I had little time to contemplate romance, however, because right away people began visiting my booth. I put my game-face on. It was time to get myself some business! I settled in behind my samples with a friendly smile on my face, ready to answer questions and dole out samples.

But after only a few minutes of talking to the crowds, a commotion caught my attention. Across the way from me I saw a paunchy man with glasses wearing a sport coat. He was locked in a heated argument with a teenager. The boy, lanky and wearing a faded band t-shirt and jeans, was gesturing wildly, his face flushed with emotion. I squinted. Sure enough, the paunchy man was my new nemesis, Councilman Weiss. It seemed the man created a stir no matter where he went.

"I hate you so much! I wish you would die!" the teenager screamed, loud enough for most of the people in the booths to turn around and gawk.

His face was red with rage, his hands balled in fists. He was a head taller and more muscled than Weiss, and my heart sped up as I watched them argue. If he chose to, the youth could easily pummel Weiss.

Instead, he stamped his foot like an angry toddler, spat out a final "you suck. I hate you," and turned and ran off through the other end of the park.

I felt a presence beside me and turned to find Brandon with his arms crossed, watching the scene as well. He shook his head. "That man. He doesn't know how to *not* make a mess of things."

"You know Mr. Weiss?" I asked as we watched the man stomp away in the opposite direction of the boy.

Brandon nodded. "For better or worse, my day job is admin to the Sugar Creek City Council. I've been working with him since he was elected. Believe me, it hasn't been a picnic." He glanced at me and then back to Mr. Weiss, who was now standing with a group near Mabel's head table. "I have plenty of experience with him. And one thing I can say is, the more time you spend around Weiss, the worse your opinion of him gets."

"Who was that he was fighting with?"

"That's his son, Jake. They fight all the time. The kid shows up almost daily to pitch a fit in Weiss's office. It gets pretty ugly sometimes."

"What are they doing here, I wonder?" I asked as I moved

around my booth to continue handing out samples now that the ruckus had cleared.

"Weiss is one of the Peachy Keen judges. All the council members are obliged to judge the festival," Brandon said with a frown. I noticed he grew angrier as he watched Mr. Weiss make his way around the booths. Looked like I wasn't the only one who found the man distasteful.

"Are you kidding me? He's judging the competition?" I couldn't believe my bad luck. The man I'd yelled at the day before would be a person deciding about whether I'd win the Peachy Keen title. It wasn't enough that he had the power to decide whether I could own a business. Now he got a say in whether I won the competition. He'd already turned my business down. This didn't look good.

Before he could continue filling me in, a group of tourists descended on his booth and he gave me a quick wave and headed back to sell his wares.

From my end of things, it felt like everything around my fledgling business was going from bad to worse. But I kept a smile on my face as I handed out samples, knowing that every person who tried one could be a potential customer. It was what I had to focus on, not the angry man that seemed to have way too much control over the fate of my business. If I focused on that, I might just sit down and cry.

# Chapter Eight

The lovely Mabel, now wearing a massive pink cowboy hat, got the crowd's attention a few minutes later by standing on a crate and turning on a portable microphone beside her check-in table.

"Howdy, y'all! Welcome to the forty-third annual Sugar Creek Peach Festival!" A whoop went up from the crowd and I grinned, a mixture of excitement and nervousness churning in my gut.

"We have eight judges this year, five from our city council and three Sugar Creek citizens. If there's a tie, Mayor Anderson will act as tie-breaker. Competitors will be judged on the appearance of the food, creativity of the recipe, how well peaches are incorporated, and of course taste! Alright, y'all! Let's get to it, the Peachy Keen competition has begun!"

I realized that Brandon had come back up beside me as I watched the judges begin their rounds. They stopped at the first booth and he leaned over. "That's Patty Larson. She's won Peachy Keen six years running. I doubt I have a chance against her, but you might just do it," he said and waved his hand toward my samples. "This is quite a bit above what I've seen here in the past. You'll put us all to shame."

The woman smiled wide at the judges as they tasted her food, and a tall lanky man next to her rubbed her back and smiled. I couldn't hear what was being said, but everyone seemed to enjoy what she had to offer. Wishing I knew what her competition entry was, I kicked myself a little for not walking around before the competition got started to see what I was up against. Then again, maybe it was best if I didn't know.

I blushed and smiled at Brandon's compliment. "Thank you, that's so kind."

He smiled back, but before we could continue our conversation, a group of women descended on Brandon's stall and he gave me a quick wave.

I continued to hand out samples as I kept my eyes on the judges. I had the competition tart samples in a warmer and I wanted to pull them out just at the right moment so the goat cheese would be deliciously gooey. A few minutes later, the judges moved to the booth next to mine and my heart constricted, knowing I'd be next. I pulled my judge samples out and drizzled the honey over them, then arranged the fresh thyme leaves with tweezers, trying to get everything just right. As I set the last tart out, they moved to me.

"Good morning. What have you got for us?"

"This is a goat cheese, peach, and prosciutto tart with thyme honey drizzle. I hope y'all enjoy!"

Each of the eight judges picked up a sample, many of them smiling and nodding at me in friendly support. A few seemed more critical, standing back from my booth with frowns, picking at the food with plastic forks. Councilman Weiss was one of them. I fretted. Had I made a mistake? Too much salt? Not enough peach? There was nothing I could do about it now but pray.

One of the judges, a middle-aged woman with a poof of blonde hair, finished her tart and licked the plastic fork clean, and then gave me a smile. She saw me eyeing the more critical ones of the group and she leaned in. "Don't mind them. They take this judging thing way too seriously. Your food is delicious."

It calmed my nerves, and I gave her a smile as the group spent a few more minutes making notes on their pads before moving on to Brandon's booth.

I took a deep breath. At least the hard part was over. There was nothing to do now but cross my fingers and wait. Oh, I wanted that title so badly. I knew it would be a huge boon for my little business. But only time would tell. I busied myself handing out more samples to the crowd and telling people about my business as I waited for the judges to finish their tasting duties and make a decision.

I watched the group out of the corner of my eye as they took samples from Brandon. He talked to them about his peach infused hot sauce and how he'd paired it with a slice of pork for the competition. When it was Councilman Weiss's turn, Brandon's smile took on a slightly mischievous edge. "And for you, Councilman, I've created a special sample." He presented a small dish to Weiss, who eyed it warily before taking a tentative bite.

Almost immediately, Weiss's face contorted in shock and discomfort. He coughed violently, spitting out the food. "What the blazes is this?" he sputtered, his voice laced with anger and surprise. "It's too hot to eat! What do you think you're doing? You and that darn hot sauce."

Brandon's smile faltered, but there was an undeniable glint in his eye that suggested this had been intentional. "My apologies, Councilman. I may have overestimated your taste for spice, given your penchant for drama," he said, though his tone suggested he was anything but apologetic.

Weiss, red-faced and coughing, tossed the sample on the ground with a scowl as he continued to spit into a napkin. "Certainly not winning anything today with this kind of stunt. We'll talk later," he grumbled and spit as he moved away, glaring back at Brandon.

I wondered what had made him do it. Brandon had seemed like a nice person, but there had been intense dislike when he had talked to me about Weiss earlier, and now I wondered just how much animosity there was between the two of them and why Brandon would have done something so cruel.

Before I could think about it much, however, there was a sudden commotion from the booth next to Brandon's, where the judges were huddled. People shuffled around and the blonde woman I'd talked to a few minutes before let out a scream. Several people backed away from Councilman Weiss as he clutched his heart and stumbled around.

He pointed to Brandon as his face turned red and then a very angry purple. "You. That awful sauce you made me eat..."

Another woman screamed as he fell backwards and hit the ground where he writhed around. Ryan and Ty immediately materialized and pushed through the crowd as a second deputy tried to angle onlookers away with little luck.

"We need medical help! Anyone a doctor here?" Ryan yelled loudly. A moment later, a young man stepped through the crowd.

"Sheriff, I got it." The man knelt and began CPR as Ryan spoke into the radio on his shoulder. "We need immediate EMT. Looks like anaphylactic shock or the like. Maybe poison. It's Councilman Weiss. Hurry."

He scanned the crowd, making quick eye contact with me and despite the adrenaline rush I was feeling watching the scene unfold, my heart bounced around wildly as our eyes met. Everyone stood around and watched as the young EMT tried to save the man with no luck.

Within minutes, the ambulance had arrived, and they got to work on Weiss as people cleared away from him. It was an awful thing to watch, and I stood back at my booth, not wanting to have anything to do with the chaos. After a minute, they lifted him onto a stretcher and carried him to the waiting ambulance.

Ryan and Ty immediately turned to the crowd and talked to

each other. A moment later, the EMT who'd tried to save Weiss came back to Ryan.

"I hate to say this, sheriff. But it looked like poison to me."

Ryan frowned, and my mind immediately turned things over. Had he been poisoned by something he ate here at the festival? What could this mean?

"Alright, folks!" Ryan called out, halting all my thoughts in their tracks. "We need anyone who saw anything at all suspicious to come talk to us." He glanced at me and frowned. "And unfortunately, I'm going to have to shut down the samples and competition. Until we can be sure that a sample didn't make Councilman Weiss ill, I can't have anyone else eating food from booths here."

A collective groan went through the crowd and Ryan shrugged. "I'm sorry y'all..." he was interrupted by the radio buzzing on his shoulder.

"Sheriff Iverson, I just had word that Councilman Weiss has passed away in transit. Need to do some tests, but it's looking like a heart attack."

Several people around us put their hands to their mouths or shook their heads. The councilman hadn't been well liked, from what I could tell, but everyone who had been present as he'd writhed on the ground gasping for air was in shock. We had just seen a man die. Possibly seen a man murdered.

Ryan turned to the crowd. "Okay, if y'all would kindly go on home unless you're part of a booth here, or unless you have something to tell me about what you saw, I'd appreciate it. Unfortunately, this year's Peach Festival has come to a close."

Frowning, I turned back to my booth. At least I'd given away dozens of samples before things got shut down. But I was sorely disappointed that I'd lost a shot at the Peachy Keen title.

I shuffled utensils around, not sure of what I should be touching. Clearly, we were all under suspicion.

"It's such a shame, honey. That tart was absolutely magical. You would have won the title for sure," the blonde judge said as she walked back by my booth. She patted my arm and as she walked away she called behind her, "but there's always next year!"

I frowned and glanced at the dog, who still sat behind my booth. I shrugged at him and he laid his head on his paws as if to say, "what are you gonna do?"

What was I going to do, indeed?

# Chapter Nine

A few minutes later, Ty began unraveling police tape and cordoning off the area where our booths were as Ryan talked to a few people who'd been present. I watched as Ty and another deputy started collecting evidence at a booth nearby where the judges had eaten, and my heart sank. Not only were they taking food from the stall, they took serving equipment and dishes from the man as well.

Moving back to my booth, I looked over my uneaten samples, unsure of what to do with all the food I couldn't sell anymore. I glanced over at the little dog and he wagged his tail a second before going back to sleep. Clearly, he hadn't been bothered by the surrounding upheaval. Cool under pressure, I liked that in a dog.

Ty continued to move around the booths where Councilman Weiss had eaten, collecting food and items that might hold any evidence. The deputy with him snapped pictures of the booths and the space around the booths. I wondered what exactly they were looking for. Evidence of poisoning might be hard to come by, especially if he'd been poisoned before attending the festival. I didn't know much about poison, though. Wasn't even sure if him being poisoned before the festival was possible.

My mind flashed back to Weiss arguing with his son. Surely he couldn't have been responsible for the death of his own father, could he? I thought about how he'd stormed off, how angry he'd seemed. Would the boy have had the opportunity to poison his father? If he had, it was probably before Weiss had judged the competition, because I hadn't seen him after their argument. Weiss had been holding a coffee cup. I wondered where it had come from. If he'd brought the cup from home, there would have been a chance. I hadn't been close enough to see if it was a takeout cup from a restaurant or something that would have come from his house, but I knew he hadn't had it with him when he'd come to my booth.

It had probably been a takeout cup from a nearby restaurant. But the coincidence of them fighting just before the man was murdered stuck in my brain and didn't want to leave. I wondered if Ryan and Ty could tell whether Weiss had been poisoned at the festival or before. If they could figure that out, the suspects could be narrowed down, whether they fit before or during the festival.

It was downright hot by this point. I was sweating through my dress, and my cheesecake samples were starting to melt into puddles. I supposed I wouldn't have gotten much more business from them, anyway. Still, the festival had turned into yet another disappointment for my business. Things weren't looking good for Deep in the Heart Catering. Not one bit.

Ty and the deputy moved to the next booth, the one belonging to Patty Larson, and the woman immediately began to wail. I frowned. What was with the waterworks? Good grief!

"I didn't do anything!" She bawled as she followed Ty around the booth as he collected her samples. "You've got to believe me. Why would I have killed him?"

"I'm sorry ma'am I'm not saying that you killed anybody," Ty replied as he swiftly bagged things up. I'm sure he was itching to get away from the drama queen. I did not envy him one bit. "I'm simply telling you that the sheriff wants me to get samples of all the food that Councilman Weiss ate. Your booth was one he visited, so I need samples from everything that you gave out."

She huffed and crossed her arms as Ty scooped her samples into a Ziploc bag and labeled them with a sharpie. He waited until the other deputy had taken pictures and nodded before turning to the next booth.

"When will I get my things back?" she cried after him.

He turned and shrugged. "I'm not sure about that, ma'am. We'll be in touch once we've processed everything."

She continued to cry, and I saw Ryan pause and watch her theatrics. I wondered what he made of it all. It was doubtful the woman would make such a scene if she truly had killed Weiss. Why draw so much attention? But you never knew about people.

Ty made his way through the rest of the booths with little fuss other than the blonde woman. Everyone else cooperated with the police without incident. Eventually, he got to the booth next to me, Brandon's booth, and I watched as he took Brandon's pork samples and then stooped to grab the paper plate Weiss had tossed to the ground, the plate that had held the spicy sample. What had Brandon been thinking, giving that to one of the judges? He must have really disliked Mr. Weiss to do something so dramatic. He had to have known he would have no chance of winning the competition. Why bother even entering, then?

Ty moved to me next and gave me a small smile as he glanced around my booth. "Hey, Abby. Gotta take some things."

I nodded and stood to the side as they made their way through my booth, bagging several of the samples that still sat out, as well as the utensils I'd used. They also took a few of the backup samples from the cooler. I sighed as Ty picked up my favorite spoon and placed it in a bag. Hopefully, the investigation wouldn't take long. I really did love that spoon. "We'll be in touch," he told me when he finished and I nodded, feeling lost suddenly. The day had turned out far different from what I'd imagined. But I was ready to get out of the heat and process all that had happened, so I turned to the job of packing my things up.

I noticed as I started to pack what equipment was left back in my box that the little dog was still lying behind my booth.

"Oh, hey there, bud." I glanced around, wondering again about his owner, but still didn't find anyone nearby. Not anyone who seemed to miss a dog, at least. It had been hours since he'd arrived at my booth, so at this point I'd be surprised if anyone came looking for him. I glanced at what samples were left on the table. They'd been in the sun a while by this point anyway, so I didn't want to serve them anymore, not that I had the chance to, regardless. But it didn't mean they weren't still good. I grabbed a couple of chicken skewers and his ears immediately perked up.

"You hungry, buddy? Want some of this?" He sat up and wagged his tail, waiting patiently for me to put the food in front of him. I smiled and slid the meat off the stick, putting it on a paper plate and then on the ground in front of him. He waited until I'd straightened back up and then dug in with gusto, wagging as he scarfed down the food.

"Looks like you're hungry. I love to see people, er, creatures, enjoying my food." I grabbed a slice of the tart, and when he'd licked the first plate clean, I picked it up and slid the second one in front of him. Just like with the first plate, he sat on his haunches and waited, this time licking his chops in anticipation.

I stood and nodded and he went in for the second portion, scarfing it down just as fast as the first. I knew my food was tasty, but this little guy really made me feel good about my cooking skills.

"I wish I knew who you belonged to." Continuing to pack up, I frowned as I got to the end of my job and still no one had come for the dog. I hated to leave him behind. He was so cute. And so hungry. He finished the food I'd given him and sat back at attention, giving me the sweetest puppy dog eyes as he licked his mouth.

"I'm going to load this stuff up," I told him. "If you're still here when I come back, I'll take you with me. But if you have a home, you should go there now." I knew he didn't understand a thing I was saying, but he settled back down in the grass like he was happy to wait. "Okay, then."

After packing the Connolys' van back up, I went back to the booth for one last check. The dog was still there. "Alright, if you want to come with me, you're welcome to. But I'm not gonna force you."

I waved goodbye to Mabel, who looked much more downcast than she'd been at the beginning of the festival, and headed to the van, the little dog following right on my heels.

# Chapter Ten

I felt like I was in shock when I pulled up to Primrose House and parked in the nearly empty parking lot. Sighing, I leaned against the steering wheel and glanced over at the dog sitting in the seat next to me. He cocked his ear, and I smiled and reached over to pet him.

"What are we gonna do with you?" I asked him. "I can't leave you out here. It's way too hot. But I don't know how Aunt Meg is going to feel about me bringing you in there, either." I gazed toward the B&B, feeling suddenly exhausted. What I really wanted to do was crawl into a bed and get some rest. But I had a van full of food to take care of, and a little dog now too.

I opened the car door and stepped out into the afternoon heat. The dog stared at me. "Come on, then," I told him and he hopped out behind me. The two of us made our way around the house to the kitchen door, where I knocked, hoping someone would be near enough to hear it.

A minute later, Aunt Meg came to the door with a puzzled look on her face. "Oh, Abby! What are you doing?" she asked me. "Why didn't you come through the front?"

I pointed to the dog, who followed close on my heels. "I'm bringing a visitor. Wasn't sure you wanted him in the house."

"Oh, who is this?" She asked me as she stepped outside. The dog moved to her and leaned into her legs and as she gave his scruffy head a pet, she laughed. "He sure is cute."

"I'm not sure. He showed up at my booth at the festival and wouldn't leave. He doesn't have a collar. I don't know who he belongs to, but I felt bad just leaving him there. It was too hot, and he liked my food." I grinned as I said it. The truth was, I really liked him. Part of me hoped he didn't have a home. Not that I had a home to offer him at present either, exactly.

Aunt Meg pulled out her phone and snapped a couple of pictures of the dog.

He cocked his head sideways and one ear bent over. It gave him a quizzical look, and I laughed. "Goodness, he certainly has personality."

"I'll put a notice up on the community and town Facebook pages, see if anyone knows anything."

She tucked her phone back into her pocket and frowned at me. "I heard about what happened at the festival. It's terrible that Mr. Weiss died there. And terrible they had to cancel the competition."

I crossed my arms and leaned against the side of the house. "It was a shame," I said. "He died only a few minutes after he ate my food. They are saying he was poisoned."

"Oh, no, that's no good. Do they know who did it?"

"Not yet. Ryan and Ty were there. They packed up a bunch of our food and things and took it off to be tested, so I guess all of us are suspects right now. The kicker is I was just fighting with Mr. Weiss in public yesterday."

Aunt Meg raised her eyebrows in surprise.

"Yep, it's true. He rejected my business license, and I got a little testy." I kicked the ground with my boot, feeling very foolish about it all now. "And then he dies right after he eats my food. It doesn't look good for me."

"Oh, but Ryan knows you would never do something like that. Don't worry about it, honey. I'm sure they'll figure it out."

I nodded and hoped she was right.

"He didn't have many friends in this town," she said as she continued to scratch behind the dog's ear. He had a silly grin on his face, and it made me smile, despite my concerns.

"I can see why. From the little experience I had with him, I knew he was a mean man. I can't imagine many people liked him."

"I wonder if it had anything to do with that bill they were trying to pass. I know he's all wrapped up in that business," she said.

"That's what I was thinking, too. Seems like a lot of people are riled up about that right now. Kind of a strange coincidence that he would die right when they're fighting about it."

"Well, I'm sure Ryan and Ty will get it figured out quick. Those boys know what they're doing."

I hoped she was right. At least this time I knew enough not to get involved in the investigation. I'd learned my lesson back in April. No more sleuthing for me. I was firmly stuck to what I did best: cooking.

"I'm sorry about the festival," Aunt Meg said. "It's too bad they won't have a winner this year. That would've been great for your business."

I shrugged. "It's okay. I gave out a lot of samples and cards, so the festival wasn't a total loss."

"Oh, that reminds me," she said. "I got some flyers made up for our dinner party. I went ahead and decided on the Saturday night after next. I hope that's good for you. I know I should've checked first, but I knew you were busy and you know how I don't like to wait on things."

I laughed. "That's okay. Luckily, I don't have any business right now, anyway. That date should be just fine."

She nodded and then gave me a funny look. "So you saw the sheriff again, huh?" she asked, a smile playing on her lips.

I blushed hard. "I did. We talked for a few minutes. But there was a lot of chaos, so we didn't have time to say much."

"And did sparks fly?" she asked.

I wasn't sure how to respond. It *had* felt like something was there still, but things had been so crazy with the councilman's death and the hubbub around the competition and the festival that I didn't know what to think. I only knew that I was still interested in him. Those blue eyes, and that curly brown hair, he looked as good as I remembered. Better even.

"I don't know yet," I told her. "Things were too crazy today. But I think we're on each other's radar." It was vague enough to stop her questions, which is what I hoped for.

"So, do you have any ideas about what you want to serve at this party of ours?" she asked.

I'd been so wrapped up in the festival that I'd almost forgotten about our party plans until now. "Nothing yet," I told her. "Although summer calls for shrimp, maybe a cold soup, some sort of salad. Peaches, no doubt. I'll stop in at Georgie's on Monday and see what kind of seasonal fair Henderson's Fine Foods has to offer. And since it's short notice, I was thinking about stopping by the bakery for the dessert portion. I could probably swing it, but it would be a lot to do by myself with the dinner as well. Especially assuming that it will be plated and served. That's going to take extra work."

"Maria and I are happy to help, and I know Jenny Abernathy's girl is looking for some work right now. She's going off to Austin to college in the fall and doesn't have a lot going on."

I nodded. "That sounds good. We'll certainly need her help. For the serving part, at least."

Suddenly, the day's work and worry caught up with me. The sun beat down on my head and I felt exhausted.

"I should probably get going," I told her. "I want to get the rest of this food put away before it goes bad. And I'm gonna have to find something to do with this dog until we can figure out who owns him."

Aunt Meg nodded and rubbed my arm. "I know it's been a long day for you already. Things will work out, you'll see. Don't worry about this death. They can't possibly think that you had anything to do with it. Ryan will know what to do."

"I hope you're right," I told her. "Oh, why don't you give me a few of those flyers you made for the party? I'll put some at Cassie's shop and maybe at the bakery, assuming Ellie is okay with it. But I think she will be if we're using her food for the dessert course."

Aunt Meg nodded and ran inside while I stared at the dog. He traipsed over and leaned into me, his tongue lolling out and a cheerful look on his face.

"What do you think, bud?" I asked him. "Do you think Cassie's gonna let you stay?" He panted and put his paw on my leg.

Aunt Meg came back out with a stack of flyers. They were pretty and well designed, and vague enough to give me a lot of leeway in what I cooked. "These look great! And I'm glad you capped it at twenty. That feels like a good number to start. Let's hope we can get that many reservations."

I gave her a hug and gestured to the pup to follow me back to the van. At least now I had some work to keep my mind off of things. Cooking was always great for that. I wasn't sure what the fate of my business would be without a license. But people seemed to like my samples at the festival, so maybe some work would come in from that.

And who knew? With Mr. Weis gone, I might have better luck getting my business license the second time around. It was a small upside to the gruesome day and although I felt bad for the man; I felt slightly more hopeful about my business. I made a plan to go back to the permit office on Monday morning, as the dog and I made our way through the parking lot.

I opened the van door for him and he hopped inside like he

belonged there. My heart went out to him. He seemed to be adrift in the world, a little like I felt in that moment. Without a solid home, or a solid business, or a solid plan. We were quite the pair. Part of me wanted to keep him, but I couldn't ask that of Cassie. I knew that on top of getting ready for Aunt Meg's party and getting my business license, I now had the chore of finding this sweet boy a home.

# Chapter Eleven

When we arrived at Cassie's house, I pulled around to park near the cottage at the back of the shop. I wasn't sure how to broach the subject of the dog with her, but I knew I couldn't have just left him behind in the park. Luckily, he seemed to be very good at following directions and didn't seem interested in running away from me, so I told him to stay at the back door to her house. He sat and cocked his head at me as if to say, "no problem, boss." I gave him a smile in a pat and then jogged over to the shop.

Cassie was wrapping a set of wine glasses for a customer when I came in through the back and she smiled and waved at me.

"Hey lady! I heard things went crazy at the festival." She eyed her customer, whose gaze had laser focused on our conversation. Clearly, she hoped to overhear some juicy tidbit from us.

"Yeah, Mr. Weiss died." The woman raised her eyebrows and leaned in. She would have found out soon enough, I knew.

"Ty called me a while ago and told me. He said they were testing all y'alls food and that the competition was cancelled. I'm so sorry, hon."

Cassie turned back to the customer and rang up her

purchase. The woman looked sorely disappointed that she wouldn't get anymore from us and reluctantly handed over her credit card.

"Take care now," Cassie said as she handed over the bag and the receipt. We waited until the woman left the store before we continued.

"He died right after he ate at my booth, Cass! Well, close to it at least."

Cassie shook her head and leaned against the counter. "Boy, you sure have a way of finding dead people."

"I didn't find a dead person this time. This time he died right in front of me!"

"Well, you have to admit, you seem to have a knack for attracting trouble of this variety."

I wish I could say it wasn't true, but this was the third dead body in less than six months that I'd witnessed. There was truth in what Cassie was saying.

"I don't envy Ryan and Ty," Cassie said, gazing at her fingernails. "It sounds like Mr. Weiss had many enemies who could have been responsible for his death. I wouldn't even know where to start."

"They are starting with all the vendors at the festival. Including me."

"Yeah, but Ryan and Ty know you. They know you had nothing to do with this."

I shrugged. "We'll see." My eyebrows shot up as I remembered the dog waiting for me. "Oh, something else. Can you come outside for a minute?"

Cassie flipped her closed sign and followed me out the back door. The dog still sat at attention in front of the cottage steps, right where I'd left him.

"This little guy attached himself to me today at the festival, and I didn't have the heart to leave him behind in the heat. I know you probably don't wanna host a dog on top of me. But would you mind if he stayed with us for a couple of days until I can figure out where he belongs?"

Cassie bent down and rubbed the dog's head, and he made googly eyes at her. He might have been a bit on the scraggly side, but he sure was good at endearing himself.

"I could probably find a collar and a line if you want him to stay outside, although it's pretty hot right now and you don't have any shade to speak of." I looked around the tiny strip of dead grass between the cottage and the shop, wondering what could be done. It wasn't exactly the best place for a pet.

"Are you kidding? Of course he can stay!" She pulled out her keys and unlocked the cottage door, opening it wide for the little dog. He panted and followed her inside and I followed too and closed the door behind us. Cassie pulled out a big Tupperware bowl and filled it with water, placing it on the ground for him and he greedily lapped up the water. She moved to a closet and pulled out a fluffy blanket, placing it on the floor by the water.

"You can stay as long as you like, you cute thing," she told him and she scratched his head.

I should've known that Cassie would welcome him with open arms. She'd always been a sucker for anything fluffy.

The dog turned twice around on the blanket and snuggled in for a long snooze, right at home. Cassie pulled out a pitcher of sweet tea and poured herself a glass.

"Do you want one too?" she asked.

"Absolutely," I told her, realizing as I looked at the pitcher of tea just how hot and thirsty I really was. With the busyness of the festival, the death of Mr. Weiss, and the company of the little dog, I hadn't had much to eat or drink all day long.

"Well, it's too bad they shut the festival down," she said as I gulped the tea down. "Seems like your business just hits one roadblock after another. What's next, do you think?"

The tea was so cold and sweet and nearly gave me a headache, but I drank the whole thing anyway and poured myself another glass. “Aunt Meg and I are planning that party. We’ve decided to do it next Saturday, so that’s something to work toward. But I don’t know what to do other than that. No business license. No Peachy Keen title. I did give out a lot of cards and samples, though.”

“Don’t worry, things will look up soon. You’ll figure it out.”

I wondered if she was right or if I had more struggles to come. Only time would tell.

“Oh! By the way, I talked to Ty about the date and he said they can probably do it Thursday night. But we’ll see with this murder. You never know what kind of work they might have with all that business. They were happy to do it, though. Ty said Ryan lit up when he asked,” Cassie told me.

I grinned. I hadn’t realized it until that moment, but I’d been nervous that he would say no. Now I had one more thing to fret about coming up quick.

“Alright, I better get back to the shop,” she told me before bending down and giving the dog one last belly rub. His tongue lolled out of his head like he was in heaven. It made me happy that he had settled in so easily. I only hoped that when we found his owner, he would want to go back home.

I followed her back out into the heat. I needed to take care of all my supplies from the festival still and get the VW van back to the Connolys. For now, it seemed that my fate was to do a whole lot of work without much reward. I mentally crossed my fingers that would change fast. The last thing I wanted to do was have to get a job, but if things didn’t improve soon, I might have no other choice.

# Chapter Twelve

The next day, I was up bright and early. Sometime in the night, the little dog had jumped up to the foot of my bed without me noticing and I found him softly snoring there when I woke. I'd gone to bed pretty depressed, but now, as I sat up and stretched in the soft morning light, things were already feeling okay again. The setbacks I'd experienced so far weren't that bad in the grand scheme of things, and I knew that focusing on what I needed to get done for the day would help me through it.

The dog lifted his head as I slid out of bed and I gave him a pet. He hopped down as I dressed and followed me out into the kitchen. I debated making coffee, but I knew Sunday was Cassie's one day to sleep in and I didn't want to chance waking her up with the smell. I grabbed my keys and motioned for the dog to follow me. We would go to Sugar Creek Bakery, which always opened with the sun.

After I gave Ellie Aunt Meg's flyers for the party and grabbed a coffee and a danish, I would take him to the pet store and find him some proper dog food. Up to now he'd only had our table scraps and my leftover samples and although I was sure he was enjoying the special treatment, I worried about how long his little stomach could stand all our rich food.

I motioned for him to follow me out to the sidewalk and pointed to a spot next to the bakery door. "Stay here. I'll be back quick as can be." Even though it was early, it was still too hot to keep him in the car. I only hoped he would stay put.

I looked up and down Main Street, also hoping that nobody would come and shoo him along. But it was nearly empty so early in the morning, so I left him where he was. The bell jingled on the door as I stepped into the bakery, and I was immediately hit with warm yeasty smells that made my stomach do cartwheels.

Ellie was at the counter, a pink apron tied over her t-shirt, her brown hair pulled back in a ponytail.

"Well, look what the cat dragged in!" she cried as she came around the counter to give me a hug. "I was so happy when your aunt told me you were coming back home for good."

Ellie had gone to school with Cassie and me. It was nice to see such a friendly face.

"Yep, I'm back for good this time!"

"I heard you're starting a catering business. If you ever want to work together on anything, you let me know. I know you can hold your own in the pastry department, but I'd be happy to team up if you feel like it." Ellie had made the cake for the wedding I'd catered in the spring. I knew she was a top-notch baker.

"Funny you should mention it," I said, pulling Aunt Meg's flyers out of my bag and handing them to her. "It's just an experiment right now. But we're planning on doing a small pop-up dinner party the weekend after next at the B&B. I hoped I could order some sort of dessert course from you, because I just don't have time to do it myself right now."

She beamed at me and glanced at the flyer. "I would love to," she told me. "And, as it happens, I have just the thing. I've been working on the special cream pastries that I think would be perfect for your party. I have one in back if you want to taste it."

"That sounds delicious. Yes, please."

A minute later, she came back out and handed over the most beautiful little tart on a paper plate. It had a shortbread crust, a creamy vanilla filling, and spun caramel sugar on top.

"You want a cup of coffee to go with that?" she asked.

"You read my mind," I said with a grin.

I bit into the tart, and it was just the right combination of sweet and salty. I'd worried that it was too heavy for a summer meal but once I tried it, I realized it was lighter than it looked.

"I could do it with berries or peaches, instead of the caramel, if that works better for what you're planning to serve for the dinner," she said.

"I haven't made up my mind about the menu yet, but I'll let you know. I'm not sure how many takers we'll get for this first one, but we're capping it at twenty to make sure we can handle this kind of thing."

She studied the flyer. "Oh, I'm sure it'll go quick. People don't have a lot of fancy options around here. And more and more there's a need for it, with all the tourists and the like coming into town."

We agreed on a price and a time for me to pick the tarts up. As I paid for the coffee, she frowned. "I heard about Councilman Weiss dying yesterday at the festival. Did you see what happened?"

I nodded. "It was right after he ate at my booth."

She shook her head sadly. "I heard they're saying he was killed. You know, he had coffee here yesterday morning, right before the festival. Hard to believe he died just a little while later."

I perked up. "He was here?"

"Yep, couldn't have missed him. He sat over in the corner with that man from Austin and they both raised their voices so loud I almost asked them to leave. I hate it when people mess with the vibe in the shop."

I nodded, totally understanding the sentiment. I hated when the vibe in my kitchen got messed up, too.

"It's awful to think that he might have been poisoned at my bakery," she said and bit her lip. "I honestly expected the cops to show up here and do a search or something when I heard about it, but nobody's been around yet."

"I don't know that they figured that much out yet. I know they are focusing a lot of attention on the booths at the festival. But I guess it would be possible that he was poisoned before he got there at all. All I know for sure is that they're looking at everyone who gave the councilman food at the festival. And that includes me."

She put her hands on her hips. "They couldn't possibly think you had anything to do with it. You just got back into town, for heaven's sake!"

I frowned. "I wish that were true. Unfortunately, I got into a little...scuffle with Mr. Weiss when he turned my business permit down the day before the festival."

She waved that away and smiled as another customer came in the door. She moved behind the pastry case to be ready for their order. "Oh, that dog don't hunt. And I'm sure Sheriff Iverson knows it. Don't worry about it, Abby. It'll work itself out soon enough."

I nodded and took the rest of the tart and coffee in my hands. "Thanks again for this. It's delicious. As soon as I figure the menu out, I'll let you know."

She nodded, and I headed back outside, leaving a stack of flyers with her to hand out. I'd saved a little of the tart for the dog, even though I sorely wanted to eat the whole thing. I was sure he must be hungry, too.

Just as I got us both situated in the car and handed the morsel over to the drooling mutt, my cell phone rang. It was a local Sugar Creek number, but one I didn't recognize. My heart jumped bounced around wildly. Could it be a customer?

I cleared my throat and answered, "This is Deep in the Heart

Catering, Abby speaking." I'd rehearsed this in my car on the drive back to Texas many times, but saying it for real made my face flush with embarrassment. It felt like I was a little girl, play-acting. I hoped it would feel more normal with time.

"Hello… Abby? My name is Brenda Weiss." The woman cleared her throat, and I thought I heard a sniffle. Uh oh, could this be about Councilman Weiss?

"Sorry," she continued, clearing her throat again. "I'm not sure if you know who I am, but my husband passed away yesterday at the peach festival?"

Oh, no. I was talking to Councilman Weiss's widow. I leaned against the seat and absently pet the dog's head. "Yes, of course. I was there. I am so sorry for your loss."

She sniffled. "Thank you. It's been quite a shock, as you can imagine. The reason I'm calling is that I was at the festival yesterday too and I had time to sample your wonderful food. I was hoping…" she paused and sniffled. "I was hoping you could bring us some food by the house for after Andy's funeral this Friday. We're having a little get together to remember him." Her voice broke at the words and I put my hand to my heart, wanting suddenly to cry with her, despite my complicated feelings for the man. It had to be incredibly difficult to lose a spouse. I couldn't imagine.

"I'll pay you, of course. The price doesn't matter. Your food was so delicious. I would love to have it there while we're remembering my sweet husband."

Huh. He must have been a very different person in her company than the one I'd interacted with. But her affection for him touched my heart.

Now, how to tell her I wasn't actually in business yet… because of her husband? I thought maybe it was best to gloss over those details for the time being. It would work itself out. I was just thrilled to be getting my first client, finally. I sat up straight and tried to channel Martha Stewart. Business maven and kitchen goddess were what I needed, not scared silly local yokel. I cleared my voice, hoping to sound professional, all the time running through what I would need to know to cater to the funeral party.

"Absolutely, I'd be happy to. About how many people are you expecting?"

"It's hard to say for sure, but maybe fifty? I'm sure you know what to do, but snacks and that sort of thing feel right, don't you think?"

"Yes, of course. Did you get one of my business cards at the festival? Could you email me and I can email you back with a quote and a menu for you to approve?"

She stalled, and I felt like I'd asked her to climb Mount Everest. "No, you know what? Don't worry about that. I'm sure you're busy. Just text me your address and the date and time and I'll be there with plenty of food for fifty. Any allergies or dislikes I should know about?"

I heard the relief in her voice. Realizing she must have a massive list of things to take care of now that her husband was gone, I filed this knowledge away and made a plan to make my process as simple as possible for clients in the future, no matter who they were or what the situation.

"No, no allergies. Okay, I'll text you the address. Thank you so much."

I hung up and grinned, nearly jumping with joy as I processed the call. My first customer! Too bad it was under such sad circumstances.

As I pulled away from the curb and started toward the pet store, I called Aunt Meg to let her know I would need the kitchen on Thursday and Friday for catering work. I wasn't happy that the man had died, but I was certainly happy to be working, business license or not. My mind flew into high gear as I thought about how I would do both the funeral meal and the party for Aunt

Meg, only one week apart. It wouldn't be a problem for an established catering business, but I was far from that. I didn't even have equipment yet. But it didn't matter. I would figure it all out.

It was exactly the kind of problem I was built for.

# Chapter Thirteen

After we left the pet store, I headed back to Cassie's house. The dog and I had ended up buying not only dog food, but treats, a squeaky toy he'd picked up, and a leash and collar. It was a lot for a dog who wasn't mine, but once I'd started shopping for him, I'd had trouble reining it in.

By the time we got back, Cassie was already over at her shop. I poured the dog some food and gave him a treat as I started thinking through what needed to be done for the funeral job. Grabbing my laptop, my notebook, and the now cold coffee I'd gotten from the bakery, I set myself up at the kitchen table. I was overjoyed to have my first client, and I wanted to get started right away on planning the food. Not only did I need to work on the plans for Aunt Meg's party, now I needed to pull off a real catering job too. But catering events was what I was here to do, and I was excited to get to work.

Since the funeral was only a few days away, I needed to focus on that first, although I also wanted to keep in mind how I might double-up on work for Aunt Meg's party. I'd never catered a funeral before, but I'd attended a few. In my experience, people often brought dishes for the family, so I was surprised that Weiss's widow would have asked me to cater for them. But it was work, and I would not question it. Besides, if the rest of the Weiss family was as poorly liked as Mr. Weiss had been, maybe no one would offer to bring them food.

I wanted to create something comforting, but upscale too. A funeral called for a comfort food, but I knew also that any number of potential clients could be at the event and I wanted to make sure to impress. Meat and potatoes of some kind would do nicely, and I made a quick list of potential pairings that went beyond meatloaf and mashed potatoes. I would need the usual vegetable and cheese platters. They always worked well with a crowd. As I scribbled notes for myself, I started a shopping list as well.

I would need some sweets too and I briefly thought about making more of the peach crumble cheesecake. But since Weiss had just died right after eating my food from the festival, one of which was the cheesecake, I thought better of it. Definitely too soon. Perhaps lemon bars and fudge would work better.

On top of the cooking that needed to be done and the shopping, I would need to gather supplies and figuring out where to store everything. I had thought about this problem briefly on my drive out, but hadn't come to any good conclusions. Aunt Meg didn't have a whole lot of space at her place for all the equipment, platters, dishes, and supplies I would need to have on hand to run a catering business. Cassie certainly didn't have any room, either. What little space she *did* have was taken up with antiques.

I realized that I might have to get a storage unit, at least for a while, until I could figure something better out. The next question on my mind was where to actually get my supplies. Up to this point, I'd mostly been borrowing or renting equipment, but now that I was in business for real, it was time for me to own my equipment and supplies.

The first place I looked was the Internet. I searched groups and lists, hoping to find someone who was going out of business or selling off supplies. After several minutes of searching, I found one restaurant in Fredericksburg that was getting rid of portable coolers. I sent the person a message asking if I could come visit and then I looked up restaurant supply stores in the area. There wasn't much around Sugar Creek, but there were several stores in Austin.

It looked like I might need to borrow the Connolys van again and make a trip over sometime during the week. It couldn't wait any longer.

Thinking about all the expenses and the work made me nervous. There was so much to do and not much time before the funeral. Not to mention, I would have to shell out a lot of money before I'd ever made any. I'd known that would be the case when I made the move back to Sugar Creek, and I'd stored up as much as I could in my last months in L.A., but still, the thought of spending the money made me sick to my stomach.

And once I was thinking about the money, it got me thinking about how much to charge Mrs. Weiss for the funeral catering. I hadn't had time to think through pricing yet, but with all of my expenses on my mind, it was the perfect time. More online research gave me a decent clue about what other people were charging in the area. Although there weren't any other catering specific businesses in Sugar Creek, several had popped up in the surrounding towns, and I knew they were my competition as much as Lulu's, or any other restaurant in town.

The cottage door rattled open, and the little dog jumped up, ready to greet whoever came in. I looked at the clock, shocked to find that over two hours had passed since I'd sat down. Cassie stooped to pet the dog and laughed when he licked her in the face.

"Hey lady, how're things?" she asked me.

"Not too bad. What about you?"

"Great! I sold that velvet couch I had in the window this morning. One of the priciest items I had in stock."

"So you decided to close up shop?"

She laughed. "I'm only open until two on Sundays. I need a little time for myself too! What're you up to?"

"Working on my business," I told her. "I got my first proper job today, so I'm trying to figure everything out."

"Oh! That's awesome! How exciting," she said.

"It is! But it's for Mr. Weiss's funeral, so it feels a little strange."

Cassie's face dropped. "Oh, that's too bad. I'm surprised they asked you to cater, since the police are looking into you for his death."

"I know. That's funny, right?" Shrugging, I and stood and stretched my muscles out. I hadn't really thought about it before Cassie mentioned it, but she had a good point. My mind turned this over. "Maybe Mrs. Weiss feels like she knows who killed him, so she trusts me. Maybe she killed him herself."

Cassie's eyes grew wide. "Whoa! I guess she could have. I wonder if Ty and Ryan have talked to her yet. I'll ask Ty."

"They must have talked to her already. I can't imagine they wouldn't have." Shrugging, I paced, my mind quickly moving from business matters to solving the puzzle of Mr. Weiss's death. "I was at Sugar Creek Bakery today," I said, "and Ellie told me that Mr. Weiss had had coffee with that lobbyist from Austin there the morning before the festival. She said that they were fighting and that she almost had to make them leave her shop."

"Oh, that's super suspicious! He totally could have poisoned Weiss, right? I mean, I don't know much about how poison works, but it seems like he could have slipped something into Weiss's coffee when they were meeting. If his wife could have done it, then so could this man."

I sat back down at my laptop and opened up a browser window, ready to do a little research. "I have no idea, but it sounds like it could have been, right? Let's see what we can find out about poisons."

Thirty minutes later, we knew a lot more about poison, but it meant little in the grand scheme of things. "So we know that he could have been poisoned any time Saturday. That's a lot of possibilities. Whoever did it knew what they were doing. Because of the festival samples, there could be any number of sources for that poison. It really clouds things."

I flashed back to Brandon and the gleam in his eye as he'd given Weiss that fiery sample.

"There was a man in the booth next to me who did something strange." I told her about what had happened, and she frowned. I didn't want to believe that Brandon had murdered the councilman. He'd seemed so nice, so genuine and passionate about his sauces. I'd been looking forward to collaborating with him before everything had happened, but now I wondered about him.

"Well, that's odd. That certainly seems suspicious, too. But what about the other council member? The one who got in a fist-fight with Weiss? Was he judging at the competition, too? He could have poisoned Weiss anytime, I suppose. If they both had access to the same food."

My eyebrows shot up. "All five council members were judges, so I bet he was! He could have totally poisoned Weiss. All it would take is one quick swipe of a sample and he could have done it. There are so many possibilities. It's a tricky one."

"Who would know this for sure? And how are we going to figure out whether or not it was him?"

I stared at her. "What do you mean, how are *we* going to figure it out? I'm not getting involved in this!"

"Oh, come on!" Cassie whined. "We could totally do some sleuthing and solve this thing. You figured out what happened to Tricia before Ryan and Ty did back in April. We could do the same with Mr. Weiss. How fun would it be if we solved the crime first?"

"I'm surprised you would even think about it, seeing how bad things went with Ty last time we tried to interfere in police business."

She waved her hand. "That's water under the bridge. He barely even grumbled."

I remembered it differently.

"Come on, Abby! Now that you've got this funeral to cater,

you could at least listen out for anything suspicious. For all we know, the killer could be at the funeral!"

She was almost bouncing with excitement. It was true; we had solved the last crime before the police could. But we'd gotten into a ton of trouble in the process and I'd nearly died. I crossed my arms and looked out the window. "Okay, we can listen out, and we can put our heads together. But I'm not doing anything questionable! Anything we find out, we're taking straight to Ryan and Ty. Okay?"

Cassie grinned. "You got it, partner! Now let's go bowling! Julia and Babs McGuire said they would meet us over at Firefly Lanes."

I glanced at my work on the kitchen table and the little dog, who probably needed to take a walk and do his business. I really should have stayed and focused, but Cassie's enthusiasm was hard to resist. "Alright, give me five minutes to walk the dog."

"Yippee!" she cried and clapped, getting the dog excited too. I sighed as I clipped the leash to his new collar. On one hand, I felt uncomfortable agreeing to sleuthing again, but on the other I was itching to figure out who had killed Mr. Weiss. Not only would it help clear my name, but I wanted to know for sure that Brandon wasn't involved. I only hoped we could stay out of trouble this time.

# Chapter Fourteen

Monday morning I was at Town Hall as soon as they opened. I hoped that the office would be more amenable to giving me my business license now that Mr. Weiss was no longer lording over the place. But I fretted I was visiting too soon, after just having been rejected the Friday before. For all I knew, they would turn me away again, but I had to try. I had a business to run.

Gina smiled at me from behind the counter as I walked into the office a few moments later, and my mood lightened considerably.

"I'm so glad you came back," she said. "I hated the way Mr. Weiss treated you the other day and I wish I would've stood up for you more."

I shook my head. "No, don't worry about it. I understand. It wasn't your fault."

"I know my business address was a problem last time," I said as I handed her the same paperwork from the week before. "But I remembered you saying there was something I could do, some clause that could get me around it? I thought that since you wanted to help me before…" I trailed off. How could I admit that I'd hightailed it over as soon as her boss passed away?

She took the papers from me with a smile. "Yes. People share business addresses all the time, so I'm not sure why it was such a problem before," she told me. "Mr. Weiss never should've rejected your application because of that." She glanced through my papers again and then smiled. "And now that I'm acting director, *I* am the one with the power to say yes or no on permits." She pulled out a stamp and stamp pad, and marked my papers with a big red "Approved," then wrote the date below it.

"Let me just make a copy of this for you," she said with a smile and moved to the back.

My heart soared with elation. I couldn't remember the last time I'd been so happy. Finally, things were starting to look up. I was so itchy to get to work I had trouble keeping myself still long enough for Gina to return.

"Good luck with the catering," she said when she came back a few minutes later and handed over my papers. "I'm sure your business will do well in Sugar Creek."

"Thank you! I appreciate it so much!" I breezed out the door on a high cloud at long last. I was in business!

Out on the sidewalk, I pulled on my sunglasses and ignored the oppressive heat. Nothing could get me down. I sauntered with a smile on my face, thinking of all the things I needed to get done next.

As I made my way down the street, I saw a couple coming toward me and recognized the man. It was hot-sauce Brandon from the festival. He was holding hands with a pretty redhead. He recognized me a minute later and waved. "Abby, hey how are you?" he said as they came up to me.

I smiled. "I'm great! I just got my business license approved."

"Congratulations! That's great news! This is my fiancé, Bianca. Bianca, I met Abby at the festival the other day. Remember I told you about the caterer? This is her."

I held out my hand and shook hers. She was petite and bubbly, and they seemed just right for each other.

"Nice to meet you. Are you a fan of hot sauce too?" I asked her.

She laughed. "I'm getting used to it, but it isn't my favorite."

Brandon got a mock offended look on his face. "We're still working on it. By the time we get married, she's going to be as crazy about hot sauce as I am."

Bianca laughed. "I very much doubt that. I could try for the rest of my life and not like the stuff as much as you do."

"Hey, I know you've been busy since the festival," he said and ran a hand through his messy brown hair. "But have you had a chance to work my sauce into a recipe? Any thoughts on collaborating?"

I hesitated, remembering Mr. Weiss reacting to the sample Brandon had given him. Even if he hadn't poisoned the man, was this someone I wanted to work with? I hated to think it, but I had my doubts.

He registered the hesitation, and his face fell. "This is about what I did to Mr. Weiss, right?"

I frowned, unsure of what to say.

"It's so sad what happened to Mr. Weiss," Bianca cut in, tension clouding her face. "Poor Brandon. He told me about the prank he pulled on the councilman. It was terrible timing. But nothing more than that. You have no idea how hard it was for Brandon to work with such a horrible person."

Tears sprang to her eyes, and Brandon rubbed her back. "Don't, honey. It doesn't matter anymore."

"It does though! He was so horrible to you!" She turned to me. "You know that the week before he died, Weiss told Brandon he should give up on the hot sauce because nobody was going to marry him with such a girly hobby? Can you believe the nerve of that man? That was just one in a constant line of abuse that Brandon had to suffer. I'm glad he's finally out of our lives."

It was a powerful argument toward Brandon wanting to kill Weiss, if it was true. Who wouldn't want to end such treatment? It would have been so easy for him to hide some sort of poison with the spice trick, too. Still, would he have called so much attention to himself if he'd poisoned someone? It seemed unlikely. I really liked Brandon, other than what he'd done at the festival. And if it was innocent, I could understand the urge to get back at someone who'd treated him so badly.

"Bianca has always been my champion," Brandon said, clearing his throat. "It's true. It was really bad to work for him, and getting worse all the time. The hot sauce prank was childish. I know it was. It wasn't my intention when I signed up for the competition, but as soon as I learned Weiss would be a judge, the thought just wouldn't leave me alone. It was a terrible decision, and I've regretted it every second since it happened. Especially since things turned out so poorly after that. He was a horrible man. But he didn't deserve to be killed."

Something about the sadness on both of their faces convinced me, despite my previous misgivings. From the little I knew of Brandon, he seemed to be a genuinely nice person, one full of passion and enthusiasm. I could only imagine what it had been like for him to be verbally abused day in and day out by Weiss. No wonder he tried to light the man's tongue on fire with his sauce.

I nodded, thinking. "I'm sure that must have been difficult to bear."

"Now the police are investigating Brandon," Bianca said, pulling a tissue from her pocket and wiping her eyes. "They had a warrant yesterday and searched our apartment. Brandon wouldn't hurt a fly. Not intentionally, at least. But now they think he killed Weiss!"

I took it as a good sign that even though I'd also had a booth at the festival; I hadn't been served any warrants. Silently, I crossed my fingers, hoping it meant the Sugar Creek Police Department considered me to not be a suspect. At least not as much of one as Brandon was.

Brandon frowned and rubbed Bianca's back again. "They will test everything and realize I had nothing to do with any poison. Don't worry, babe. Not to mention that I just filed a complaint against Weiss the week before he died about the working conditions. Why would I have done that if I was planning to kill him? It would have made me look even more guilty, right? And why would I have made such a spectacle of myself? I'm sure after they put the pieces together, they will realize that it wasn't me. That I'm just stupid and silly."

He shook his head, raising his eyes back to me. "It's a mess. But it'll get cleared up, eventually. I'm sure they'll figure out who killed him. My money is on Greg Roblais."

"Who's Greg Roblais?" I asked.

"He's the lobbyist that supported Weiss's campaign. He was around the office a lot. Those two just wouldn't quit. As soon as Weiss won the election, they started fighting."

Now that he mentioned it, I bet Brandon knew all kinds of information about Weiss's business dealings on the council. I didn't want to pry, but I couldn't help myself.

"What was the lobbyist doing around town still? From what I read online, it looked like he supported Weiss's run for office. But that went through a while back, right?"

Brandon shrugged. "Yeah, but the lobbyist supported Weiss so he would push this franchise bill through. And Weiss had changed his mind about that. I don't know why, other than just because he could. Boy, he liked to mess with people. I wouldn't be surprised if he went back on his word just to antagonize Roblais. So Roblais would come around regularly, I'd say once a week or so, and just poke at Weiss, remind him of his promises. They would meet behind closed doors, but there was plenty of yelling, anyway." Brandon shrugged and ran a hand through his hair.

It was an interesting tidbit, but one I had no idea what to do with, although it did trigger thoughts about what Ellie had said. Brandon wasn't the only person who'd seen the two men fighting. I tried to shake it all off, though. Now that I had my business license, it was time to go full steam ahead, turning my little catering company into something grand. I smiled at the couple.

"Don't pay any attention to me," Brandon said as he blew out a breath and then gave me a smile. "It's all water under the bridge at this point. I'm trying hard to push all thoughts of Weiss out of my mind, but it's been difficult. I spent a long time being tortured by the man. I'm sure the cops will figure it all out, though. We should probably get going. It was good to see you, Abby! I really hope you'll consider working with me. Don't let that little incident at the festival convince you otherwise."

I smiled at them both. "Okay, I won't. It was good to see you. Nice to meet you, Bianca. I'm sure I'll see you around."

Walking toward my car, I couldn't keep the smile off my lips. Deep in the Heart Catering was a real business. It was a good day.

I caught a glimpse of Brandon and Bianca turning the corner as I slipped into my steambath of a car and frowned. I wanted to believe him, and what he said made a lot of sense. But it was hard to forget how much glee had been on his face as he'd watched Weiss choke down his food at the festival on Saturday. Could he have poisoned Weiss? It was hard for me to believe. You never could tell about people, though. I'd found that out the hard way back in April. I shrugged and turned the car on, hoping to push the thoughts of murder and suspects out of my mind. It was time to get to work.

# Chapter Fifteen

I spent two very frustrating days tracking down supplies everywhere from Sugar Creek to the opposite side of Austin, but by Thursday morning I finally felt ready to cater the funeral. I was working with the bare minimum as far as equipment was concerned, but it would have to do until I started making a little money. At least I'd used the driving time over to Austin to work out the details of both menus in my mind, and I felt like I knew what I needed to do to make the events happen, hopefully without a hitch.

After I got the dog squared away for the morning at Cassie's house, I headed to the grocery store. I'd debated borrowing the Connolly's van again, but it seemed like too much effort. But once I left the store with all my goods for the funeral, I regretted my decision. I stuffed bags and boxes of food into my car every which way until my Honda was packed to the gills. It was so crowded in my little car that I had to put a shopping bag full of lettuce on my lap as I drove over to Primrose House. I prayed that nobody I knew would see me in such a state.

It wasn't exactly business like.

Luckily, it was early, and I made it through to the other side of town without embarrassing incident. I finally peeled myself out of the car at Primrose House and grabbed as many groceries as I could and headed for the kitchen door, where Maria met me with a smile.

"It looks like you could use some help," she said.

I nodded a grateful smile and the two of us shuffled food from my car to the house in the quickly rising heat. Ten minutes later, we had things as put away as possible and I pulled my apron on to get started on the prep work. One of my Austin purchases had been a small refrigerator, which we'd squeezed into a corner behind the door. At least this time I wouldn't have to stress as much about where to store my food, unlike when I was here back in April. Lack of fridge space had almost cost us the wedding, and I would not let that happen again.

"Good morning, honey! Woo, good thing you bought that extra fridge!" Aunt Meg said as she came into the kitchen with a cup of coffee and surveyed the disaster that had once been her kitchen.

I nodded. "Yeah, got a lot of work to do for the funeral tomorrow. Thanks again for letting me use the kitchen."

She waved her hand at me. "This kitchen is as much yours as it is mine. Think of it as your business too. Speaking of which, we've already got three signups for the party, a total of seven guests!"

"Wow, that's fantastic! And fast. We're nearly halfway to full and have more than a week before the event. Those fliers must be doing their magic."

Aunt Meg nodded and sat at the bar stool to watch me work. "People have been asking about the menu and I've been playing it off like a secret, but it sure would be nice to tell them something when they ask. I don't suppose you've had any thoughts."

I grinned at her as I pulled out a cutting board and shuffled the produce around.

"As a matter of fact, I do have some thoughts. A lot of thoughts, thanks to Ellie's delicious cream tarts. I want to do a cold cucumber or carrot soup to start. For the second course, I was thinking of grilled shrimp with a green goddess salad. For the main course, I'd like to do a choice of steak or fish with a summer panzanella salad and grilled vegetables. And of course, we'll have Ellie's tarts."

"Oh my goodness, girl, you are making me hungry! I might need a snack!" She laughed and reached over to a carton of strawberries I'd put on the counter nearby and snagged a couple. "Now that I know what I'm selling, I bet I'll get those other seats filled in no time."

I nodded as I sharpened my knife. "Oh, I also want to get a couple of cases of the Connolys wine to serve, a mix of white and red. We'll probably need a few beers too for the ones who won't want the wine. Do you want to get it or should I?"

Aunt Meg frowned. "I think you'd know better which wines would pair with the food you're making. I bet if you told them what it was for, Mark and Sheila would do a private tasting for you, even!"

That sounded like a fun idea, one I might have to pull Cassie in on. The thought crossed my mind to invite Ryan and Ty along, but I immediately nixed the idea. The last thing I needed when trying to make a business purchase was a distracting male presence. And as soon as I thought about Ryan and Ty, I grew flustered. Our double date would be this evening, and I was a bundle of nerves thinking about it.

"Alright, well, good luck in here today. I've got a few guests I need to attend to, but I'm around if you need me. And Maria would be happy to help too! I know she's been excited about the catering side of things, so don't hesitate to ask her!"

Aunt Meg left me alone in the kitchen and I got to work. It gave me a little time to think in peace about what I needed to do for the day. Luckily, Cassie was at the shop, so she planned to let our new canine companion out for a few bathroom breaks throughout the day, but I hoped that the prep work for the funeral wouldn't take me too long. I wanted to leave myself some downtime to relax, and shower, and to steel my nerves for our double date.

The first thing I started with was dicing shallots. I would need a lot of them for the bruschetta I planned to serve, but also for the meatball sauce. To make the bruschetta, I would need to slice a whole lot of baguette into thin slices, mix the topping, and then right before the event tomorrow, top all the little toasts with either a mix of tomato, mozzarella, and basil, or peaches and mint on top of a thin spread of ricotta, and drizzle them all with a balsamic glaze. They were a cheap option for a crowd, but a bit on the labor intensive side right before an event, so I planned to pair them with a few dishes that could be done ahead of time like meatballs and cheese and veggie trays to balance my work load.

After I finished with the shallots, I decided to get the fudge done. Fudge, with its rich, velvety texture, was always a hit, and making it a day ahead would allow its flavors to deepen beautifully. I combined sugar, cocoa powder, and whole milk, stirring gently to blend everything into a smooth, chocolatey mixture. The kitchen filled with a warm, sweet aroma as I turned on the heat and let it come up to a boil and then let it sit at a boil for a very long time, stirring it occasionally. When it got close to finishing, I stirred in a pile of chopped local pecans and vanilla extract.

During that process, Maria came back in. "I'd love to help if you have something for me to do."

"Do I ever!" I gave her a bag of potatoes that needed to be peeled. "Thank you so much."

After boiling the fudge sauce, I added a generous dollop of butter, letting it melt and merge into the mixture. Once it got to just the right consistency, I stopped stirring and let it bubble away, its surface shimmering like a chocolate mirror dotted with nuts.

I let the chocolate cool a bit before pouring it into a prepared pan and smoothing the top with a spatula. It would harden over the next hours and I would cut it tomorrow morning before the event.

"The party you and your aunt are planning is an excellent idea," Maria said as she placed the potatoes in a massive pot of water and turned it on to boil. "The guests will like it. I was thinking I could take some pictures of the event and put them on our website. I did some photography back in Mexico and I think I could do a decent job if you want me to do it."

"That would be great," I replied. "I've been thinking that Primrose House could do with more marketing efforts. Quality photos would go a long way. I have an old friend from college that works for a paper in Austin. I was thinking about giving him a call and seeing if you wanted to do a writeup of the place for their travel section. I know the customers are out there. We just need a way to reach them, tell them about how amazing Primrose House is."

"I love your aunt, and I love this job. I will do whatever I can to help out here and keep Primrose House going." There was emotion in her voice and it made me realize that Maria was as attached to this place as Aunt Meg and I were. Her livelihood depended on us being able to keep things going. It gave me even more motivation to work hard on our plans.

"I know the feeling," I told her. "Don't worry. We'll figure everything out. Luckily, we have a crew of strong, smart women!"

We continued to work on food prep and talked companionably as the day flew by. At some point Aunt Meg came back in, poured us all a glass of iced tea, and sat at the counter to keep us company.

"So, I heard through the grapevine that you have a date tonight."

My cheeks flared, and I scowled. Darn Cassie. She could have kept quiet.

"It's true."

Aunt Meg eyed me over her glasses for a long moment.

"Should be interesting to see the sheriff again. Wonder if they'll have anything to say about Mr. Weiss. Speaking of which, how does it feel to be catering a funeral for Mr. Weiss?" she asked as she flipped through a copy of Better Homes and Gardens.

I stared at her a minute, amazed that she'd let the date conversation drop so easily and then shrugged. "It's a little strange. Especially since he died so soon after eating at my booth. But I'm trying not to question it so much. A job is a job!" I just hoped that the guests wouldn't pay me too much attention. The last thing I wanted was to get into any scuffles over the Councilman's death. Hopefully, I would blend in, get treated like the help that I was.

"I bet there'll be all sorts of characters coming out of the woodwork. His death has caused quite a stir. Lots of people have ideas about who killed him. It isn't just you and Cassie snooping around," Aung Meg said with a laugh.

"We aren't snooping! Not really." I shrugged and mashed the boiled potatoes together with plenty of milk and butter.

Aunt Meg glanced at me over her glasses. "Uh, huh. And I'm the Queen of Sheba. I know you girls. You can't stay out of this."

I frowned as I scooped the potatoes into a massive mixing bowl and added cheese, sour cream, eggs and freshly chopped chives and mixed it all together the best I could with a wooden spatula. It took a whole lot of muscle power to plow through the mixture, but eventually I got it all combined fairly well and scooped it into mini muffin trays. I would store them like that until the next morning, when I would pop them into the oven. They would puff and crisp and create delicious little morsels of potatoey goodness.

"Well, I might keep my eyes and ears open. You're right, the funeral is going to be interesting, if nothing else," I said.

"You better tell the sheriff if you find anything, though. No more Lone Ranger antics from you."

I'd thought she'd forgiven me for my stunt with Janine Yardly back in April, but clearly there were still some unprocessed feelings about it all.

"Don't worry, I learned my lesson!"

"Good." She laughed and nodded and then got a funny look on her face. "You know, sharing a little clue here and there with the sheriff might be a good way to deepen a relationship. Keep on his good side, keep in his line of sight."

"Aunt Meg! Please!"

She laughed again. "Oh, honey. Don't worry, you and that sheriff belong together. It's clear as day, right Maria?"

Maria laughed and nodded as she sliced through a loaf of baguette.

"If you two don't stop this, I'm going to find another kitchen to use. I don't want to discuss my love life while I'm working. Thank you very much," I said.

"Okay, okay. We're sorry. Don't get all huffy," Aunt Meg replied.

I threw a cube of cheddar at her, and then we all had a good laugh. But the thought had stuck firmly in my head. Whether Cassie and I decided to sleuth on this thing or not, it might be good to keep an eye out for anything I could share with Ryan. If nothing else, it would give me something to talk to him about, which right now I could really use. The thought of our looming date made my heart skip a beat, and I picked up the pace in the kitchen, realizing it was almost time to get ready. I just hoped I would survive this date so I could work the next day.

# Chapter Sixteen

A little before seven, Cassie and I pulled up in front of a swanky restaurant in downtown Fredericksburg.

"I thought you promised me low key," I complained as we got out of the car and made our way inside. I'd heard of the place. It had been on Texas Monthly's up-and-coming restaurant list recently. Definitely not low-key.

Cassie shrugged and frowned. "It's a date, Abby. It's not like I was going to set it up at a burger joint."

I frowned and tugged at my dress, feeling flustered and frustrated. "A burger joint would've been fine with me."

She ignored my complaints and turned to talk to the hostess as we stepped inside. I felt bad for complaining, but as I looked around, the candlelight and the soft music felt a lot more romantic than I'd hoped for. As much as I was interested in Ryan, I was shy about our budding relationship, unsure of where we stood. And this date suddenly felt like a great big leap when I'd only been ready for a tiny step.

"It's okay, Cass. I'm sure it'll be great. I'm just nervous," I told her when she turned back to me.

She smiled and gave me a hug. "You look great in that dress. Ryan's going to fall head-over-heels."

Before I could respond, the door swung open and Ryan and Ty entered the restaurant. There was a decidedly male presence to them, and my heart skipped a beat as my nose caught a whiff of aftershave. They were both dressed in slacks and button-down shirts rather than their usual uniforms, and both men looked very good all cleaned up.

"Sorry we're late, we had something come in last minute that we had to look over."

Cassie and I gave each other a wide-eyed look. Boy, did I want to know what had come in. I wondered if there was any way we could weasel it out of them.

A hostess showed us to a lovely corner table. The room had high ceilings and perfect mood lighting. It felt very fancy, and I tried my best to focus on the menu rather than on the man next to me. If I focused on him, I might swoon.

"How's the catering going?" Ryan asked me when I finally put the menu down.

"It's okay. I finally got my license. And I've got a job tomorrow, so things are going well, despite the setback of the festival."

"I'm sorry about that," he said.

"She's catering Councilman Weiss's funeral!" Cassie told them.

Ryan raised his eyebrows. "That's interesting."

"Isn't it? I'm surprised his widow asked me, but I guess she tasted some of my food at the festival." I shrugged just as the server came to take our orders.

After ordering our dinners, I said, "I know y'all can't tell us anything police business related. But have you finished testing the festival things? Any chance of getting my things back soon?" I wanted to know when I would get my favorite spoon back. But I also wanted to know if they'd learned anything. I wanted to know why they'd searched Brandon's place. But that was far too nosy of a question, so I kept my prying vague, hoping they'd let more slip.

Ryan nodded. "That's what held us up this evening, actually. We got several reports back. All the sample testing from the festival, as well as the autopsy."

"Did you find anything?" Cassie asked as a server portioned a bottle of wine into our four glasses.

Ty and Ryan glanced at each other, sending a signal I couldn't read. "Nothing definitive."

"Abby heard Weiss was fighting with someone at the bakery before the festival. It sounded like it might have been that lobbyist from Austin. We thought maybe he was the one who poisoned Weiss. Maybe he put it in his coffee?"

"Sounds to me like you two are trying to play detective again. That didn't turn out well last time," Ryan said and took a sip of the wine.

I flushed and frowned at Cassie. The last thing I wanted was to get into trouble again, especially on a date.

Ryan's eyes met mine. "I can get your stuff back to you tomorrow. Sorry we had to hold it for so long. I know you had nothing to do with the poisoning, but it's procedure."

"Thanks, I'd appreciate that," I replied.

"So, you think the Austin lobbyist could have killed him?" Cassie asked, not willing to let it drop. I nearly kicked her under the table.

"Cassie, honey. Y'all need to stay out of it," Ty said.

Cassie blew out a breath, exasperated. "Why? You know we have access to information that you two simply don't. People in town are much more willing to talk to the two of us than the two of you. We could team up, help out. For starters, Abby could keep her eyes and ears open for y'all at the funeral tomorrow. Get some good dirt that the police might not be privy to. We're on your side, gentlemen. Don't you see that? We are a great resource."

"I don't think we should discuss..." Ryan began.

"Oh, please! You two know we aren't going to say anything!

We are helpful! Abby was the one who figured out what happened with Tricia..." Cassie interrupted.

Ryan cut her off, putting his hands up in surrender. "Okay! Okay, dear Lord. Let's not go down that rabbit hole again!" He hesitated with a final glance at Ty. "We got the autopsy report back. Weiss was definitely poisoned at the festival, not before. Because of the type of poison, we know it was from one of the booths he ate at. So it wasn't the lobbyist."

Our food arrived just then, and I took a moment to appreciate the beauty of the plate. Perfectly seared scallops sat on a bed of satiny risotto dotted heavily with porcini mushrooms and artichoke. I took a bite and closed my eyes. The scallop was perfectly cooked and covered in a lemony sauce that was to die for. It was so good I almost wanted to go in back and talk to the chef, try to pry away his or her secrets.

Ryan caught my eye and smiled. He dug into a porterhouse steak with creamy potatoes and asparagus with gusto. "I'll give you some of mine if you give me some of yours," he said after taking his first bite.

He was a man after my own heart. I nodded and smiled, and we shared a little of our food with one another.

"So what you are saying is, Weiss was absolutely poisoned by one of the booths where he ate competition food," Cassie said, returning to the conversation after we'd all had a few moments to enjoy our meals.

"Or someone who had access to booth food. Luckily there's a camera over the plaza, so we have a solid list of who was and wasn't in the area during the competition tasting. The bad news is that the list is very long, as you can imagine," Ty said.

I nodded and sipped my wine, trying to process it all. But the quiet glamour of the restaurant, the dancing candlelight, and the rich wine all started to go to my head. I stole glances at Ryan when he wasn't looking, taking in his long lashes, his large capable hands, the dimple in his cheek when he laughed. I wanted to think about the implications of what they were sharing, but my head wasn't in the game. Taking a long drink of water, I tried to clear my mind.

"I saw Weiss fighting with his son before the festival. Was the boy one of the people on your list?" I finally asked.

Ryan shook his head. "No, I saw that argument, too. Jake Weiss left before the competition even began. He's not a suspect. We tested all the booths, but nothing came up from any of them. So whoever did it, they hid the evidence very well. Not a trace. My guess is that whoever it was had some sort of eyedropper of poison and got hold of one of the councilman's samples when nobody was looking."

"I talked to Brandon White the other day. He said that you'd searched his place. You think it could have been him?" I asked.

"We had an anonymous tip, as a matter of fact," Ty replied. "Hope it wasn't you two this time?"

I rolled my eyes. "I hope you know that Cassie and I learned that particular lesson. Don't you worry, if we find something out, we're coming straight to you with it."

"Is Brandon a suspect?" I asked again.

Ryan gazed at me for a moment, his thoughts indecipherable.

"I'm only wondering because he wanted to work with me on something. I'm trying to decide if he's worth the risk. I didn't like how he pranked Weiss."

Ryan cleared his throat. "Brandon is not under investigation for the murder. He's been cleared. The prank was a bad idea, but we're fairly certain that it wasn't what led to the councilman's death."

I sighed, relieved that my instincts about the hot sauce aficionado had proved correct, at least as far as any of us knew.

Before Cassie and I could pry any further into the investigation, the server came to offer us dessert. I was stuffed, but the description of a molten lava cake with cherry sauce had everyone in a tizzy. We decided to share one for the table.

"So Ty tells me you're staying at Cassie's place for now. Do you have plans to get your own place after a while?" Ryan asked as we waited for dessert to arrive.

I nodded. "I'm not sure when, but yes. It depends a lot on how the business goes. Right now, I'm bleeding money all over the place. But I'm lucky to have such a great friend to put up with me."

"I hope she never leaves," Cassie said with a laugh.

Ty frowned and grumbled something under his breath and we all laughed as dessert came.

The chocolate cake was heavenly and even though I felt like I couldn't eat another bite, I scooped up my share of the decadent oozy chocolate and cherry, thinking about how great a combination it was.

At last, the check came and after a minute of haggling over it, we let the men split it. Walking out into the warm evening a few minutes later, Ryan's arm brushed mine, and I felt a chill run up my spine. It had been a lovely night, much more enjoyable than I'd imagined.

"It was good to see you tonight," Ryan said and leaned in for a hug. A thrill passed through me as he wrapped his arms around me. "I'm glad you came back, Abby," he whispered into my neck.

"I am too. It's good to be home," I replied.

"My schedule is up in the air right now because of this murder investigation," he told me as he slowly pulled away, "but I was wondering if sometime next week you might want to come over for dinner at my place. You don't have to cook!" he said with a laugh. "I didn't mean that. I can grill us some steaks. Make a salad. What do you think?"

I smiled and nodded. "Sounds like fun. Why don't you give me a call when you're ready to do it? I'm catering this party at my aunt's B&B next Saturday, but otherwise I'm free."

I turned toward the car with a smile as wide as the Brazos, my heart beating a mile a minute.

"Oh, Abby?" Ryan called. I turned back.

"Make sure to let me know if you hear anything important at the funeral tomorrow." He smiled and waved.

I nodded and waved back, trying hard not to trip over my feet as I floated back to the car.

# Chapter Seventeen

Friday morning was draped in a heavy grey, the skies above Sugar Creek adding to the somber mood of the day. Even with the cloud cover, the heat was oppressive, but at least we would get a break from the relentless summer sun. The Weiss home was located in the wealthier part of Sugar Creek, where sprawling yards were green despite the heat of summer and fancy facades and fountains decorated nearly every residence. As I pulled up to the address that Brenda Weiss had texted me, I found a long driveway that split in two directions, one part to a loop at the front, and another a straight line around the side and back of the house. I pulled down the straight lane, guessing it would lead me to the kitchen.

What hit me first was the massive amount of plants that took up every available space on the Weiss property. Shrubs and trees fought for space, a massive variety of vines wound through fences and up trunks, and ground cover carpeted every inch that wasn't the driveway.

Someone had a green thumb. Goodness.

As I got out of the van, I confirmed my suspicions about the kitchen location as Brenda Weiss stepped out the side door wearing a black shift dress and black hose. Her nose was red and her hair was piled in a bun on top of her head. She sniffled and pulled out a tissue, waving me over.

"Oh hello, honey. Good timing. You can come through here," she motioned to the door she stood in. "You need some help? I'll get Jake to help you."

"Oh, no!" I told her as I pulled out the first of many cooler bags I'd brought. "I've got it..." but stopped when I realized she'd already left. I shrugged and hefted the cooler to the side door, where I nearly collided with the boy who'd been arguing with Mr. Weiss before the festival.

"Mom said I should help." He was sullen, angry, hunched and wearing a suit with a loose tie. I knew the feeling of losing parents too young and my heart instantly went out to him. No matter how much he disliked his father, he must be in a world of pain right now.

"Oh, it's okay, I can manage," I told him.

"It's no problem, Ma'am. I'm pretty strong. You got something heavy I can carry?"

There was pride beneath the pain, and I gave him a smile. "Sure, give me a minute and I'll find something."

I put the bag down and went back out to the van, opening the side door and pulling a large cooler to the edge. "This is pretty heavy," I told him. "You want some help?"

He grinned and leaned into the cooler, easily hefting it. "I got it."

"Wow, you're pretty strong. Do you play sports?"

"Football. Got a scholarship to A&M," he replied. There was anger in his voice again. It must have been a sore spot. I opened the door for him and he set the cooler down on the floor.

"I'm sorry about your father," I told him as he straightened and met my gaze. At my words, he looked away, his face turning dark once more.

He shrugged. "It's fine."

I put a hand on his arm. "It's not. I know. I lost my parents when I was a kid."

His eyes turned back to me, sympathy in place of the anger. "I'm sorry."

"It's okay. It was a while ago. But I know how it is, that's all."

He frowned. "We were fighting right before he died." Tears sprang to his eyes, and he crossed his arms. I nodded, encouraging him to continue, but otherwise I didn't dare move a muscle, knowing just how hard it probably was for him to open up. I would listen for as long as he needed me to.

"It was so stupid. He was the one who wanted me to go to A&M. He forced me, said I was wasting my life wanting to stay in Sugar Creek. But I have a life *here*. I have a girlfriend and we're in love. She's not done with school yet, so if I left for college I'm worried she'll find someone else. Mom understood. Mom was always on my side. But Dad didn't want to hear any of it. He said women are a dime a dozen." His voice cracked at the words. "And that I needed to man up and take charge of my life. He never really cared about what I wanted. But it doesn't matter now, because he's gone."

Tears fell then, and I reached for a tissue and handed it to him. He wiped his face angrily, clearly uncomfortable with the level of emotion he was sharing with me, a total stranger.

"I gotta go," he mumbled and headed out of the kitchen. I wished I could give him a hug or say something kind. He seemed like he needed a little kindness in his life. But that wasn't my job. My job was to feed hungry and grieving people. And so that's what I focused on.

The Weiss kitchen overflowed with plants as well. Orchids, ivy, house plants in every shape and size imaginable took up counter and floor space. I frowned, trying to decide where to put all the food.

I pulled two serving platters of bruschetta out of the big cooler and put them onto the marble countertop. Fruit and cheese platters came next, and I arranged everything around the dips and dried fruit and adjusted the pieces that had fallen out of place. I set out tasteful high-end plastic wear and napkins and then arranged the chafing dishes on a side counter that would hold the warm food, lighting the burners after filling the basins with water.

"Oh, this all looks so lovely," Brenda Weiss said as she came back in the room with two flower arrangements a few minutes later, shoving them between the houseplants on the side table. "Thank you for doing this on such short notice."

"I'm happy to. And thank you for taking a chance on my business. You said you tasted one of my samples at the festival?"

She smiled and nodded, but there was something cold in her eyes that made me uncomfortable. I continued to fiddle with the burners as she watched me.

"A delicious cheesecake. Not something I normally eat, but it felt like a day to throw the rules out the window." She gazed over the food I'd already put out. "Don't suppose you have any more of that?"

I shook my head. "Sorry. But I do have fudge and lemon bars if you're looking for something sweet."

She gazed out the big picture window that looked out over an absolute jungle in the back, a swimming pool just barely visible beyond the patio amidst all the foliage. "Little did I know that day would be my husband's last day on earth. It all seems so unimportant now. He'd been under so much stress lately," she said, almost to herself. "With that bill he was wrapped up in, and that man always hounding him. Night and day, pressuring, arguing. I thought he'd have a heart attack with the stress of it all."

I was very quiet, and still, silently pleading that she would continue to talk. Her voice cracked, and she clutched a handkerchief tightly. "But now he's dead. And from a heart attack, not because of the stress, but because someone poisoned him!" The last words were whispered, a sob catching in her throat, her mouth turning down. Before I could reply or console her, she left the room.

Could she have killed her husband? I really started to wonder. I wouldn't be surprised, especially as I thought about what Jake had told me, that his mother had supported him even when his father didn't. Could she have killed him to give her son the freedom he so craved? I didn't know enough about the family to know for sure, but it seemed a good enough reason as any.

I busied myself with the finishing touches as I heard people beginning to come into the front of the house.

Showtime.

In no time at all, the kitchen was crowded with people in varying shades of black and grey. They talked amongst themselves as they piled food onto plates. Some of them brought dishes of food into the kitchen. I was happy that at least some people had a community spirit and happily helped them slide their casseroles and piles of cookies between my own food.

Many of the guests looked familiar, but it had been so long since I'd been a regular in Sugar Creek that I didn't know most of them by name. I listened in on their conversations as hard as I could while still attending to the food. Luckily, once I'd put out all my food buffet style, there wasn't very much for me to do other than to tidy and replenish, so I could turn some of my attention to sleuthing. Not that I meant to go full hog, but Ryan *had* said he wanted to know if I heard anything, so I felt like my nosiness was sanctioned.

Most of the talk had nothing to do with Weiss's funeral. Several people commented on how tasteful the ceremony had been. I heard a few whispers about how the bill was sure to fail now, and how the rest of the council must be mighty happy to have Weiss gone. But nothing that seemed important to figuring out who killed him.

At least until a tall older man came in and the room fell into a hush. He frowned, and I noticed a nearly healed bruise on his face.

A woman with a shock of red hair standing near me leaned into another woman. "That's Councilman Landers. He was the one fighting with Weiss last week. Mabel told me she thinks he killed Weiss."

The other woman gasped. "And now he has the gall to show up to the funeral? How tacky."

They moved off, and I studied the man as he made his way around the buffet, picking at food but not taking very much. So this was the man who'd fought with Weiss about the bill. I vaguely remembered him now from the festival, but I'd been so busy at the time and so focused on my anger at Weiss that I hadn't paid him much mind until now.

He certainly acted uncomfortable. I wondered if there was any truth to what the women had said. It would have been easy enough for the man to slip something into one of Weiss's samples. After he left the kitchen, the bustle and talk picked up. I was surprised by how everyone had reacted to him. Either the common line was that this man had killed Weiss, or something else was going on that I didn't know about.

I turned my focus back to my work as the disturbance from Landers subsided. The day flew by and the atmosphere of the house enveloped me—a mix of hushed voices and the faint, floral scent of sympathy bouquets. A little over an hour into the funeral gathering, I leaned against the counter during a lull and gazed into the backyard.

I stood straight when I spied Brenda Weiss out on the patio with a man in a suit I'd never seen before. The two of them were clearly arguing, Brenda Weiss stabbing at his chest with her long red fingernail. Part of me wanted to go out and see if I could help, or if I could snoop. But I also knew that it would immediately move their focus onto me, and that was the last thing I wanted. If they realized I was involved in any way, it wouldn't be good for me. They might even ask me to leave. So I kept still and watched them argue.

Could this be the lobbyist from Austin? He certainly seemed slick, not much at all like a local. Although that didn't mean much at the end of the day. I'd been gone too long to know who was and wasn't a Sugar Creek resident any more.

Brenda Weiss turned on her heel and stalked toward the door. I quickly turned and busied myself so she wouldn't catch me staring. She came in and slammed the door, growling and out a breath as she moved quickly to the front room.

A moment later, the man came inside and I tried my hardest not to stare him down, but I really wanted to know who he was. He ran a hand through his hair as he looked toward the front room and then realized I was standing nearby. He gave me a slick smile and glanced over at the food.

"Looks good," he said, although he didn't grab a plate.

"I'm Abby Hirsch," I told him, extending my hand. Normally I wouldn't have introduced myself to a guest, but I was burning to know who this man was.

He stared at my hand a moment before taking it. "Greg Roblais."

So here was the lobbyist, and at the funeral of Councilman Weiss, no less. How very interesting.

Before we had time to talk any further, though, a commotion from the front of the house interrupted us. Raised voices and a crash had me rushing out of the kitchen to see what was going on.

# Chapter Eighteen

The front room was a combination sitting and dining area, an enormous space with floor to ceiling windows and a high ceiling. Wood floors were covered in very expensive and old looking rugs. Guests were everywhere, on the couches, at the table, standing against the walls. Brenda Weiss sat crying in the midst of it all, in the center of a very white couch, staring in anger at a couple near the drink cart in the corner. With a start, I realized it was Patty Larson and the man who'd been with her at her booth during the festival.

"How dare you two vultures come into my house on a day like today," Brenda said to them, "and start talking about the property line? This is not the time or the place. My husband is barely in the ground!"

A broken cocktail glass lay at Brenda's feet. I was itchy to go clean up the mess, but every eye in the room was on her, so I held my ground. As soon as the altercation was over, I'd clean up.

"I knew this funeral would be exciting! See, Ted, aren't you glad we came?" an elderly woman whispered to a man near me.

The man with Patty straightened and slugged back the rest of whatever had been in his tallboy. "Brenda, you and I both know that you couldn't give two hoots about your husband being in the ground."

A collective gasp rippled through the room. Hoping to be as unobtrusive as possible, I headed back to the kitchen to grab a dustpan and hand broom. Might as well get ready to pick things up. But also, I wanted to position myself near Brenda in case things got ugly. One of the jobs of a caterer is very often diffusing tension borne of too much alcohol at parties. It wasn't my favorite thing to do, but I could do it if I had to.

I came back in just as Brenda stood from the couch, her heels sinking into the plush carpet under her, the glass crunching with her steps. I winced. That wouldn't be easy to clean up. "I want you two to get out of here right now. I don't ever want to see your ugly faces again!"

"Can you believe the nerve of those two?" one woman asked as I passed her to pick up empty plates on a coffee table. I collected used napkins and dishes and placed them on the tray I'd placed in the corner for that very purpose, trying to stay out of the way while watching the altercation.

"Come on, Chad. We don't want to be here anyway," Patty Larson replied, tugging at her husband's sleeve. "Please, don't make a scene." She seemed very uncomfortable, and I wondered what her role in everything was. Funny that she'd also been responsible for causing a scene at the festival.

The man shook her off and laughed. "I guess now that Weiss is gone, I'll have no trouble getting that property line issue fixed. Just you wait, Brenda. You *know,* the people over at the permit office can't wait to get back at Andy. They'll approve my request as soon as I put it in. Expect the fencers next week."

Brenda lunged at the couple, and Patty dragged her husband quickly to the door. Thank goodness I wouldn't have to step in. Chad Larson was a big man, and I honestly wasn't very confident that I could have done anything to stop him if I wanted to.

As soon as Patty walked out the door, however, she let out a shrill cry and we all ran to see what was the matter.

---

On the ground near the front steps a man in a suit writhed on the ground. I peered over someone's shoulder and immediately realized that it was Greg Roblais.

I didn't even hesitate, but pulled my cell phone out of my pocket and called 9-1-1. Guests poured out onto the front lawn to gape at him as he struggled in pain. Within minutes, an ambulance had pulled into the drive and the EMTs had the man on a stretcher. He was still moving as they put him in the back of the ambulance, his arms flailing wildly, nearly hitting the EMTs. I prayed he wouldn't meet the same fate that Weiss had just days before. The similarities between what had happened to Weiss at the festival and what was happening to Roblais were hard to overlook.

I looked around to find Patty and Chad Larson, but didn't see them anywhere. They must have gone home finally. But it was strange that they hadn't stayed to see the drama like everyone else who crowded around the yard.

"Who was that?" someone asked as the ambulance pulled away.

"That guy from Austin, the one who was causing all the trouble! Looks like he won't be causing any more trouble now."

He'd looked just like Andy Weiss had looked after he'd been poisoned at the festival, and my mind raced. This was not good. Not good at all.

Whoever had poisoned Weiss had likely just poisoned Roblais as well. And used my food to do it. I was hopping mad, and scared as all get-out. This wouldn't look good for me, the caterer who served food to two people who were poisoned. It didn't matter that I was innocent. It wouldn't take long before popular opinion turned against me.

"Nobody eat another thing!" I heard Brenda Weiss shout from behind me, right as I had the thought. "The food's poisoned." She turned her gaze on me then, the meanest glare I'd ever had directed at me in my life. "It was you, wasn't it? You killed my husband! And poisoned Mr. Roblais!"

The surrounding crowd murmured and started to get angry. People crowded around me and suddenly I was afraid for my life. It felt like a mob was about to descend. It was boiling hot, and I yanked at the neck of my chef coat as people started to press in, making me sweat.

Thankfully, at that moment, Ryan and Ty pulled up in their cruiser and jumped out into the fray.

"Okay, folks, let's calm down and back up a bit, please, if y'all would be so kind," Ryan said as he and Ty walked toward the group that was quickly surrounding me. The crowd began to back off, but they still felt very threatening.

He got close enough to grab me if needed and then turned to Brenda Weiss on the steps where she lorded above us all. I fought the urge to lean into him.

"What seems to be the problem here?"

"That woman, that caterer!" Brenda said with a sneer. "She was one of the people my husband ate from at the festival before he died. And isn't it the coincidence that she's here feeding people when somebody else dies from poison?"

"We don't know yet that anyone else has died," he corrected her as he glanced at the angry faces all around.

"She must be guilty, Sheriff Iverson! It makes sense!" someone to the left of me said.

I shook my head. "I would never! You have to believe me! I just got to town!"

The crowd began to shout at me and shake their fists. "Murderer!" Someone cried.

"I don't want to die, Mommy," a boy said nearby. "Did she poison me too?"

"That is enough, everybody!" Ryan shouted over the noise. He said it with such power that the entire group quieted. He was quite the presence when he wanted to be. The perfect person for the job of sheriff.

Ryan frowned and crossed his arms, deep in thought. He bent his head, the brim of his cowboy hat shielding his face from the sun that had appeared as we'd stood outside.

Finally, after what seemed like forever, and with a look of anguish on his face, he turned to me. "I'm sorry, Abby. But I'm going to have to have you come with me."

I fought the urge to crumple into a heap right there on the ground. Tears sprang to my eyes. How could he do this to me? Surely, he knew I would never poison anyone. I couldn't believe that this was happening to me.

"Ryan, no," I begged him, trying to make eye contact with him, but he wouldn't meet my gaze.

"Ty," he said as he gently put his hand on my arm to lead me to the cruiser. "Can you collect food samples? Get a little of everything. I'm sorry folks, but the party is over. Go on home. And if anyone feels ill, make sure to get right to the hospital."

"You should check the drinks, too. I don't think Roblais had anything to eat." I said it loud enough for everyone to hear, not that they would care now what I had to say. But if I could cast a little doubt about my guilt, it would be worth it. Not to mention, it was true. Not only had he not come in while I'd been manning my food stations, I remembered the disinterest in the food he'd had when he'd introduced himself to me in the kitchen earlier. Maybe he was one of those strict food diet weirdos. Who knew?

Ryan nodded to Ty. "She's right, test drinks too. Whatever empty glasses are sitting around."

I doubted they would find anything. Just like at the festival, there was simply too much churn, too many possibilities for someone to poison a drink or a scrap of food without evidence.

I turned to get one last look at Brenda Weiss as Ryan guided me toward the cruiser. I could have sworn she was smiling.

# Chapter Nineteen

At least he had the decency to open the door for me before guiding me into the back of the cruiser.

"That was totally unnecessary. I would have come to the station if you'd asked me. You didn't have to haul me away in front of everyone. Unless you think I really did it?"

I slipped onto the leather seat, my heart beating hard, in anger or fear or both I didn't know. The metal bars separating me and Ryan were real and cold. I could not believe what had just happened to me. Not only had I been publicly humiliated and accused of murder, I'd been arrested by the man I was starting to fall for. Life couldn't get any worse. I was sure of it.

Ryan slid into the driver's seat and started the engine. He turned and looked back at me.

"I didn't have a choice, Abby. Those people were gonna come after you if I didn't take you in. You know they would."

I ignored him and stared out the window, my heart breaking. My business was never going to get off the ground now that I'd been taken away by the police. Now that I'd been accused of murdering people with my food.

Ryan turned forward and sat thinking a minute longer before

pulling away from Brenda Weiss's house, as if he wanted to say more. But he was silent as we glided down the long drive. I watched the people out my window angrily glaring at me, and it was all too much.

Tears poured down as we drove through the neighborhood and I thought about how completely ruined everything was. I knew Ryan meant what he said, but the fact that he'd taken me away in his cruiser rather than sticking up for me was too much to bear. I wasn't sure I would ever forgive him.

"It's just procedure, honey. Please don't cry. I know you didn't poison anybody."

I finally turned my gaze to meet his and glared. "It doesn't matter. Everyone back there thinks I did. Deep in the Heart Catering is toast. Nobody in this town will ever hire me to cook food again."

"That isn't true, and you know it. Once we figure out who poisoned the men, we will clear your name and no one will have reason to doubt you."

"Ha! You and I both know that's a bunch of bull. Or maybe you haven't been in a small town long enough to know, Mr. Dallas." My voice turned cold at the last point. I was digging myself into a hole, but I couldn't help it. I wasn't even thinking straight anymore. "People will remember this forever. The story will get distorted and nobody will remember the *details* after a while, but everybody will know that Abby Hirsch is someone you don't ever want to hire."

He pulled around to the back of the station and parked, then turned to look at me. "I know you don't believe me right now, but things will work out. Ty and I are working hard on this thing. And now that the second man was poisoned, it helps to weed out suspects considerably. We know the killer had to be present at both the festival and the funeral. We know it has to be someone who is connected to both Weiss and Roblais. And we know it isn't you."

His eyes were soft and despite myself, I felt the tiniest bit of forgiveness creep in.

"Come on, let's go inside. You can tell me everything you saw at the funeral and then you can go home."

He got out and opened the door for me. I hesitated, mad as a hornet still and not wanting to cooperate. But the seat was awfully hot, and I had to go to the bathroom. I scowled as I got out and followed him a pace apart, refusing to look at him.

I wondered about what he had said, that he hadn't had a choice about arresting me. Could things have gone differently? I thought back to the angry mob nearly attacking me, about how scared and threatened I'd felt when he'd arrived. And I knew that despite my anger, the anger that wouldn't subside anytime soon, Ryan had indeed done the right thing back there.

"I need to pee," I told him as we walked through the back door and into a long, dreary hallway.

He took me to the door to the restroom and crossed his arms. "Don't get any funny ideas about running away." It was a small smirk that crossed his lips, but I saw it.

I hit him in the shoulder, hard. "I can't believe I ever kissed you."

He rubbed his shoulder, but his lips crept up into a smile. "I'm sorry, Abby, honey. I'm just trying to lighten the mood."

"Don't you 'honey' me. Not the time, Ryan. Read the room." I slammed the bathroom door in his face.

Ten minutes later, we sat in his office, going over everything that I could remember about the funeral. I told him about Brenda arguing with Roblais. I told him about her strange comments and my thoughts about how she might have killed her husband to protect her son. I told him about the Larsons causing trouble and then disappearing after finding Roblais. I hadn't forgiven Ryan for arresting me. I wouldn't do that for a while. But he was right. The faster this murder was figured out, the faster I could at least clear my name and start to rebuild. I wasn't sure if it was possible, given what had transpired over the day, but after a few hours away from the situation, I had found a tiny scrap of hope.

"So you're saying that Brenda Weiss fought with Roblais before he was poisoned? And that the Larsons were there causing a scene?"

"And that the other council member was there, the one who got in a fistfight with Weiss. I didn't see him when we found Roblais outside. He might have left by then, but he was at the party earlier."

Ryan crossed his arms and paced the room. "It rules a few people out for me, but it doesn't make things much less complicated. I hadn't really thought about Brenda being a real possibility before today, but the way you describe her actions, it seems more likely."

I wasn't sure if he was opening up more about the case because he felt guilty about how things had gone, but it was good to be hearing some of his thoughts about the case finally. Now, more than ever, I wanted to figure out who killed Weiss.

Ty popped his head in a few minutes later. "Boss, got a call from the hospital. Roblais is going to survive. Doctor Wilkins is on the phone and wants to talk to you for a minute. The toxicology looks like a match." He smiled at me and nodded shyly. I scowled back at him and he ducked quickly out of the room.

"I'll be right back," Ryan told me, leaving me finally alone with my thoughts. Other than the quick bathroom break I'd taken earlier, I'd been with people all day long. With Ryan most of the day. I needed time alone to process and to think. I was still seething with anger at him, but what I really wanted to think about was the poisoning. Who could have done it?

Brandon was definitely a no. I'd figured that out as soon as I'd talked to him, and Ryan had confirmed it, but he also wasn't at Weiss's funeral party so that ruled him out completely. The council member seemed unlikely as well, although I knew little about the man. In my mind there were two prime suspects after what had happened at the Weiss residence, either Brenda Weiss or one of the Larsons.

I thought about their public bickering about the property line. It seemed like an old wound, and I wondered how long the two couples had been at each other's throats.

I wondered too about the motive. I could see it easily for Brenda, at least as far as Weiss. She was protecting her son from her husband. And she'd seemed so angry at Roblais when she talked about him and when they'd been on the porch fighting that I could easily see her poisoning him too, even though I didn't know the why behind it.

The Larsons were much more of a mystery. Weiss's death made sense because of the property fight. But what motive would they have for trying to kill Roblais? Did they even know him?

Ryan came back in, interrupting my thoughts. He set a cup of coffee in front of me and patted my shoulder. I shrugged his touch away, but only half-heartedly. I knew I wouldn't be mad at him forever, but he'd certainly hurt me and I wasn't forgiving him anytime soon.

"Roblais is going to be fine. He was poisoned with the same poison as Weiss. So that tells me we very likely only have one poisoner. I thought that was probably the case, but now I have the proof."

Suddenly the door burst open and Cassie came flying through it in a huff, her curly hair flying, her sunglasses still on.

"You should be ashamed of yourself, Ryan Iverson," she said.

"Cassie, please do not start. I was only trying to protect her."

Cassie glared at him and then pulled me up out of the chair and wrapped her arms tight around me. I sank my head to her shoulder and cried all over again.

"It's okay, lady. Let's get out of here. These fools don't deserve our tears."

She took my hand and guided me out of the station without a backward glance. Once again, my best friend had come to my rescue. What would I do without Cassie Divine?

# Chapter Twenty

Cassie sped us back to Primrose House as the sun set. "Your aunt and Maria came over to the Weiss house with me as soon as Ty told me what happened. We took care of everything for you, washed the dishes, put things away the best we could, although I'm sure nothing's where you want it," Cassie told me with a shrug as she pulled into the parking lot at the B&B.

I'd been so busy and so worried since Ryan had taken me to the station that I hadn't even thought about all my catering supplies and cleanup at the Weiss house. I must be in some pretty serious shock. I normally would have had a conniption thinking about so much unfinished business. Thank goodness I had a posse of lovely helpers.

We pulled into a parking spot just as the sun sank completely and got out of the car. "Thank you so much. I don't know what I'd do without you," I leaned in to hug her but I was stopped when Aunt Meg opened the front door and the little dog came flying toward me, yipping and running with all the intensity and speed of a tiny cheetah.

I laughed as he jumped around me and barked. I was so overcome with everything that I sat right down in the gravel drive and let the little guy hop up in my lap and lick my face. I was laughing and crying at the same time, my emotions all knotted up like a tangled ball of yarn.

"Oh, Abby. I'm so sorry," Aung Meg said as she stopped in front of me and held out a hand to help me up.

I took it after giving the dog one final hug and then stood, dusting off my dirty jeans.

She pulled me into a big hug and a second later, Cassie came up behind me and hugged us both. And then I felt a third set of arms around me and realized that Maria had followed Aunt Meg out and embraced us all, too. I laughed and hugged them all back and the dog bounced around us and barked. It had been a terrible day. One of the worst since my parents had died. But the love and care I felt wash over me in that parking lot made it all sting a whole lot less.

We all walked back into the house after a minute, arm in arm, the dog weaving around us.

"You decided to let the dog come inside, I see," I said to Aunt Meg as we walked into the cool front room. The air conditioning felt delicious after the evening heat.

"He's so well behaved, and Cassie needed to go get you. I didn't want to leave him outside. It's too darn hot."

We all went into the kitchen. Maria moved to the refrigerator and grabbed a bottle of milk, and then put a heavy pot on the stove. "I know just what you need," she told me with a smile. Although I wasn't feeling much like eating or drinking, she was so kind that I held my tongue and let her make me whatever she wanted. She added dutch cocoa, sugar, cinnamon sticks and vanilla extract to the pot and brought it to a simmer.

"It's a special cocoa recipe from my grandmother."

As soon as she said the word cocoa, the little dog perked up from where he lay over by the kitchen table and yipped.

I cocked my head and looked at him. Everyone else stared at him, too.

"Looks like our new friend like's cocoa too." As soon as I said it, he jumped up and came over to me. Sitting, he put a paw on my leg.

"That's funny. He seems to like the word cocoa," Cassie said, and then laughed when the dog bounced to her.

"Is your name Cocoa?" I asked him. He lunged at me and yipped again, and I laughed.

"Cocoa! Of course you are. You look just like a Cocoa." He danced around excitedly and we all laughed.

I moved to the fridge and after a minute, found a Tupperware of leftover meatballs I'd saved for him before the catering gig. His eyes grew wide, and he sat at attention as I held one up for him. "Hey, buddy. Is your name Cocoa?"

He wagged his tail and licked his lips. I wasn't sure if his name really was Cocoa or he just really wanted a meatball, but I laughed and gave him one.

"Looks like one problem is solved, at least," I told the women. "He's got a name! And it's one that both suits him and suits us. What could be more appropriate for a food business than a dog mascot named Cocoa?"

Cassie laughed and grabbed a meatball, too. She held it out to him. "Come here, my little Cocoa Puff." The dog trotted to her and took the meatball from her fingers carefully. We all laughed.

I sat back down, feeling lighter, and watched as Maria turned the burner off and poured four mugs of delicious cocoa, setting one in front of each of us and then taking the final stool. We all bent over our cups, the rich cinnamon aroma enveloping me. My shoulders began to relax and only then did I realize how tense my body had been all day.

"This is incredible," I told her as I sipped. I hadn't wanted it, but I sure did need it. Rich and smooth, it settled my stomach and soothed my heart.

"Okay, tell us what happened," Aunt Meg said. "We heard the basics from Cassie, but I'm sure Ty didn't tell her all the details."

"Roblais was poisoned at the funeral. He didn't die, thankfully, but Brenda Weiss accused me of poisoning him and her husband in front of everyone and I was nearly mobbed. Then Ryan showed up and more or less arrested me in front of everyone."

"I cannot believe the nerve of that man," Cassie said as we sipped our cocoa. "He should know better."

I frowned and fiddled with a coaster in front of me. "He said he did it to protect me. I was so mad at him when he did it, though. I could just see all those people staring at me being taken away in the police car, thinking that I was a poisoner. It doesn't matter if I clear my name. What people saw is what's going to stick in their minds. I think my days of catering in Sugar Creek have come to an end. And after only one official event." I rubbed my hands over my face. I was all out of tears, but I sure felt like bawling again.

"I'm sure Ryan was only doing what he had to. I know he cares about you and wouldn't have done it if he'd had any other choice," said Aunt Meg.

"That crowd really was pretty vicious," I replied. "They scared me. I wish there would have been another way out of it, though."

"You can't let this get you down, honey," Aunt Meg said. "I know things look bleak right now. But it will blow over, you'll see. The police will figure out who really killed Weiss and poisoned Roblais, and the town will move on."

Cassie frowned and shook her head. "No. What we need to do is to solve this thing for ourselves. We are smart and we have a lot of resources. We could figure it out if we wanted. Probably faster, just like last time."

Aunt Meg glared at her, but I perked up. Suddenly I felt much more inclined to sleuth than I'd felt a few days before. Cassie was right. We *had* solved Tricia's murder faster than he had. Why not this one too? I started poring over the day's events, thinking back through anything I missed as I formulated some ideas.

"My prime suspect right now is Brenda Weiss. It's strange that she would have asked me to cater the funeral party after what happened at the festival, but then it was a perfectly convenient way to shift the blame onto me. She seemed downright giddy when Ryan took me away." I scowled, remembering her smug face as Ryan had escorted me to the cruiser.

"I could see why she would have killed her husband. I can't imagine having to live with someone like him. But why would she have tried to kill Roblais?" Aunt Meg asked.

"I saw them arguing at the funeral. Who knows what they have between them? There could be any number of reasons. Or maybe it was completely to finger me for the murder. He didn't die after all. Maybe she was just trying to move blame away from her and onto me."

"It's strange she would have done it at her own house, though. Especially during something so public," Maria said.

I shrugged. "It creates a lot of chaos and a lot of possible suspects. The other council member was there, the one Weiss fought with. And the Larsons were there too, the Weiss's next-door neighbors who also had a booth at the festival. They were arguing with Brenda about some property line issue."

"But would either of them have a reason to go after Roblais? I guess the council member might have some motive with the lobbyist, but I doubt the Larsons even knew him," Cassie said.

"That's a good point. I guess we just don't know enough right now about Roblais to understand the motive there. That would be a good place to start. We could also find out more about Brenda, see if we could get some dirt on her and Weiss or her and Roblais. Figure out if there's a motive there."

All of a sudden, I was utterly exhausted. It had been a long, grueling day. I slumped in my chair and Aunt Meg noticed.

"Okay, ladies. It's been fun, but I think our girl needs some good shut-eye. We can talk more about this tomorrow."

I thanked Maria for the cocoa and she vowed to give me the recipe. Then Cassie, Cocoa, and I headed out to Cassie's truck.

Aunt Meg followed us out and just before I stepped outside, she grabbed my arm and pulled me back for another hug.

"Abby, honey. I know it's hard to imagine, but after a while you won't be so angry at him. It was horrible that he had to do it, but you know he didn't have a real choice. Those folks would have skewered you if he hadn't taken you away. If anything, he was kind of like a knight in shining armor."

I frowned, unwilling to give him such leeway.

Aunt Meg patted my arm as I pulled away. "I know you're hurting and you're angry. It was a terrible thing that happened to you today. It's right to be hurt and angry. But after a good night's sleep and a little time to think, things will start to look better. I'm sure of it."

I hugged her back, grateful for her positive energy, even if I wasn't feeling it myself. I only hoped she was right.

# Chapter Twenty-One

The next morning, Cassie and I drank coffee on her small front porch as we watched Cocoa chew a bone bigger than his face in the grass patch between her cottage and the store. Aunt Meg was right. A good night sleep had helped. I wasn't completely over what had happened the day before, but this morning I felt more positive. Feeling some hope about looking into things with Cassie went a long way in that direction. I wasn't sure it was the smartest thing to do, but it certainly felt the best.

"So, what's our plan going to be? How are we going to figure out who killed Weiss?" Cassie asked.

"I'm not sure. We definitely have several angles we need to look into. Brenda Weiss is on top of my list, but I want to know more about the councilman too since he seems to have the best reason of anyone to have wanted to poison Roblais. At least that we know of."

"Ty is coming by the shop to have lunch with me this afternoon, and I'm going to press him for whatever details I can get out of him. I'd especially like to know what kind of poison was used on Weiss and Roblais. Knowing that would help a lot."

I nodded. "Absolutely. The way I see it, we need to figure out motives and we also need to figure out how both men were poisoned. I'm almost positive that Roblais didn't eat any of my food yesterday, so it was likely in a drink. So whatever the poison was, it had to have been something that could've been in either a drink or food and in a small enough portion that didn't leave behind any trace. Unless they found some evidence at the party. Which they could have."

"I'll see what Ty will tell me. They might not know yet, though. I know those tests can take a while," Cassie said. "I'm not sure how we're going to learn more about Brenda, though. She isn't exactly in our social circle."

I sipped my coffee, looking out over the morning, and then I sat up straighter as I remembered Brandon. "I bet I know someone who has some information. Brandon White works with the council members and he knew a lot about Weiss and Roblais, probably Brenda, too. He wanted to talk to me about working together on something having to do with his hot sauce. It would be a great opportunity to pick his brain. I'll reach out to him today."

"That's a great idea," Cassie replied. "So we both have something to work on as far as our sleuthing career is concerned."

I gave her a skeptical look. "This is not a career. This is a single mission to clear my name."

She laughed. "I know, I know."

We finished up our coffee and after giving Cocoa a healthy dose of pets and water and food, Cassie and I left for the day. She drove me over to Primrose House to pick up my car, promising to be in touch after her lunch with Ty.

I needed to look through my supplies and do some organizing after the event the day before, so I headed inside after she dropped me off. Everything about my business was up in the air, and I didn't even know if the party we were planning for the coming Saturday was still going to happen, but I decided I would act as if it was, and get some work done.

Better to plan for a party that doesn't happen than to host a party without a plan.

Maria was in the kitchen when I arrived, packaging up leftover food from the B&B breakfast trays.

"Good morning," she said. "Are you feeling better today?"

"Much better, thank you. I just wanted to check out a few things and see what work I need to do to get ready for Saturday."

As I said it, Aunt Meg walked into the room. "I'm glad you're here," she told me. "I hate to have to tell you this, but we had two cancellations for the party from locals overnight, so we're back down to three reservations. Two are from tourists, but the third is Councilman Landers. Seems he either doesn't care about what happened yesterday or he hasn't heard about it yet."

"That's strange though, don't you think? Seems like most of the town's heard by now. Maybe he just hasn't had time to cancel yet."

It was disappointing to hear we'd lost customers, but not that surprising. Honestly, I was happy to still have anyone signed up at all.

"I think I'll go over to Fredericksburg this afternoon. Spread a few flyers around at some of the other wineries in the area and let them know about our catering company and the party. You never know what might lead to more reservations."

We still had a week before the party was scheduled to happen, so my hopes weren't completely dashed. Still, I would have to work hard to get enough reservations to make it worth our while.

I moved to my catering fridge and rifled through the contents, making a few notes as I went and thinking about how to approach Brandon with my questions, which got me thinking about his hot sauce. Going into the pantry, I shuffled things around for a minute before finding the jar of hot sauce he'd given me. I twisted off the lid, poured a bit onto my finger, and tasted it again. It was spicy, but it was also deliciously sweet and tangy with a hint of peach, and I thought about how great it would be on grilled shrimp or meat. Because I planned to serve shrimp at the party on Saturday, I started there.

Pulling frozen shrimp from the freezer, I thawed it quickly in water as I mixed up a seasoning of oil, garlic powder, hot sauce, and salt. Once the shrimp were defrosted, I tossed them in the sauce and then threw them in the oven on a high heat to quickly roast.

B&B guests shuffled in and out as I worked, getting coffee and snacks and complementing the smells in the kitchen. When I finally pulled the tray out, several people had gathered, all wanting to try my creation. I gladly doled out shrimp to whoever wanted one and asked for the feedback. Mostly, I wanted to know if it was too spicy. I could always adjust anything else, but the hot sauce was the real question. The reaction I got from the guinea pig guests was positive, so I decided to use the recipe for our dinner party.

It was a good enough place to start, at least. And it gave me something to talk to Brandon about besides my snooping. I pulled my phone out and texted him to set up a time to meet. We agreed to meet at Ellie's bakery in an hour.

---

When I arrived at Sugar Creek bakery, it was crowded with tourists and locals alike. Sweetness and baking smells hung in the air and it made me hungry. I got several stink eyes from the locals, but I ignored them and made my way up to Ellie and ordered a blueberry muffin and a cup of coffee.

"Hey, I heard about what happened yesterday. I'm so sorry," she said, her face showing concern as she handed over my order.

"I was worried you would believe it and not want to do the desserts for the party anymore."

"Are you kidding?" she asked. "There's no way you poisoned anyone." She said it loud enough that several people turned towards us, curious about our conversation. She waved a hand at them and a few had the decency to look away. "They'll realize it, eventually. What reason would you have to poison some lobbyist from Austin? I've seen him in here with any number of locals, but you didn't even know him."

I perked up at this. "I know you said he was fighting with Weiss the day he died, but I wasn't aware that he was a regular."

She nodded. "It didn't seem that important at the time, but yeah. He was in here often, meeting with people. Council members, business people. I guess since he was from out of town, the bakery seemed like a good enough office space without the hassle of paying." She rolled her eyes.

"Did he ever meet with Brenda Weiss here?"

She frowned and looked around the bakery, trying to remember. "She and her husband met with him a few times. But that was back before the election. Oh! Brenda and Roblais also ran into each other a couple of weeks back. They got their coffee and took it outside. I thought it was coincidence, but now that you mention it, it could have been an actual meeting."

"Was it heated? Or friendly?"

"It seemed friendly enough, but I honestly didn't pay much attention. There's a lot going on around here most days. I'm lucky if I can pay attention to the work in front of me," she said with a laugh. "Speaking of which, how are things going with the party for next weekend?"

"Unfortunately, we've had a few cancellations," I told her.

She shrugged. "I'm sure you'll fill it up without problems. I'm still planning on making the tarts for you, so don't worry about that."

I nodded. "I think the peach ones would do best for what I'm planning to serve, if that's still an option. And thanks for believing in me," I told her. "It means a lot."

She grinned at me. "Are you kidding? I know your business is going places and I want you to use my bakery! I'm looking forward to the increased business!"

Just then, Brandon walked in and I waved him over. He ordered a cup of coffee and we sat at a corner table near the window. It was bright and a little warm, but pleasant enough.

"So, you've had a chance to think about my hot sauce," he said as he blew on his coffee.

"I have. I'd like to add it to a recipe for the party we're hosting at Primrose House next weekend. I did a few tastings this morning with the guests there and got some good feedback. My plan is to list it on the menu along with the name of your company, and if you'd like to, I can have a few jars for sale if anyone wants to take it home. I bet it would do great with the tourists. They're always looking for something to take back with them."

Brandon grinned from ear to ear. "That sounds fantastic. Thank you so much for taking a chance on me, especially after what happened at the festival." He blushed and looked down at his cup of coffee.

I shook my head. "Don't worry about it. Seriously. I'm just glad you wanna still work with *me* after what happened yesterday."

He met my gaze again. "Yeah, I heard about what happened at the Weiss funeral. I'm so sorry."

"It was a shock, that's for sure. I didn't even know Roblais, so I'm not sure why anyone thinks I poisoned him." I shrugged. Here was my chance to get some dirt, and I went in for the kill. "Do you have any thoughts about who might've done it? I didn't know Roblais, but *you* did. Did you see anything that might be a clue as to who would've killed him when he was in visiting Weiss?"

He sipped his coffee for a bit, thinking. "I know he met with several of the council members over the last few months, not just Weiss. He was really trying to push that bill through, but nobody seemed to want to budge in his direction."

"Did Councilman Landers meet with him, the one who got in the fistfight with Weiss before he died?"

Brandon nodded slowly. "He did, but I don't know why. Landers was staunchly against the bill. At least that's the ticket he ran for office on. He never would've wavered as far as I know, so I don't know why Roblais would have bothered to meet with him at all."

"What about Brenda Weiss? You think she could be responsible?" I asked him.

He frowned and nodded. "It could've been her. She liked to play the loving wife, but I heard them arguing plenty when she visited him at the office. I'm not sure about why she would try to kill Roblais, though. But surely they knew of each other. He was constantly in Weiss's ear and they must've done fundraising and that kind of thing together before he was elected to the council. But I'm not sure what motive she would have to kill him, especially now that Weiss is dead."

It was a good point, and one I couldn't quite figure out. Unless maybe there was some sort of blackmailing or secret that I didn't know about, which was perfectly possible. Probably not something Brandon would know either.

"I honestly don't know who makes the most sense," Brandon said as he finished his coffee. "So many people disliked him, but not that many people knew Roblais, so the crossover makes it difficult. Unless Roblais was a cover-up or some way to shift attention away from whoever is guilty. I just don't know."

I nodded and thanked him for his time when he checked his phone. I didn't want to keep him longer than necessary.

"I'll get the bottles of sauce over to you in the next couple of days, and maybe some signage too if you're okay with it," he told me as we stood. "Do you want me to bring them by the B&B?"

I waved goodbye to Ellie and then we stepped out into the afternoon sunshine and I squinted in the bright light. "Sure, that or Cassie's shop. Either is fine. I have enough to cook with for the party, so it's no rush, but definitely get them to me by Friday so I can get them set up. And whatever signs or literature or anything like that you might want to include is great, too."

"Thanks again," he told me with a smile and a wave. "I really appreciate you using my sauce in your business. Don't worry about the thing that happened yesterday. Take it from me. Once the public eye shifts, they forget pretty quick. My prank with Weiss is already old news. What happened at the funeral will be soon enough, too."

We headed our separate ways, and I hoped he was right because I did not like the limelight. Not one bit.

# Chapter Twenty-Two

I spent the rest of the day visiting wineries and breweries between Sugar Creek and Fredericksburg. The places were hopping with tourists, and despite the downturn in things for me lately, I couldn't help but be hopeful as I passed out flyers about our party. Several owners seemed to like the idea and promised to send people our way.

By the time I got back to Cassie's house late that afternoon, I was pooped. Cocoa greeted me with friendly yips and jumped up on the couch next to me as I plopped down. I pet him as he licked me all over, happy to have someone to hang out with again. I let myself have five minutes to relax before getting up to take him on a walk. I knew he needed to go, but my exhaustion was soul deep.

Cassie's shop stayed open late on Saturdays, so after resting for a while, I moved to the kitchen and rifled through the fridge, trying to come up with a plan for dinner for us. Because I'd been so busy with the festival and the funeral the last week, I had done little cooking for us since I'd arrived, even though it had been my intention to pull my weight in the kitchen in return for Cassie putting me up.

We didn't have much to work with, but I couldn't bring myself to go to the grocery store, so I did a little brainstorming and decided on a minestrone soup and quick bread. I got to work chopping onions, carrots, and celery as I thought about the things I had learned throughout the day.

Between information from Ellie and Brandon, I had a lot to mull over. My prime suspect was still Brenda Weiss, even though I didn't know what her motive was, at least for poisoning Roblais. She was present at both the festival and the funeral. Brenda also knew Roblais in some capacity and she could've easily planned to invite me to cater in order to pin me with suspicion for the poisonings.

A knock on the door pulled me out of my thoughts. I rinsed my hands and wiped them on a towel before going to answer it. In the week I'd been living with Cassie, we hadn't had a visitor, and I wondered why anyone would come here rather than her shop.

As soon as I opened the door, I had my answer. Ryan stood there in jeans and a light blue t-shirt, several of my cooking supplies in a box in his arms. I hated myself for noticing how the color of his shirt brought out the beautiful blue of his eyes.

"Hey, Abby," he said, his voice deep and hesitant.

Cocoa yipped and ran out the door, dancing around Ryan, eager for a pet from the new stranger. *Traitor.*

"Who's this little guy?" he asked. He handed me the box of supplies and bent to pet Cocoa, who leaned into him. Whatever Cocoa's strong suits, a guard dog, he would never be. I set the box down on the entry table and stuck my hands in my pockets.

"We aren't sure. He came home from the festival with me and nobody's claimed him yet. Aunt Meg put notices up but no word. We're calling him Cocoa. He seems to like it."

The dog rolled over on his back, begging for a belly rub, and Ryan bent down lower with a laugh and rubbed his belly.

"Thanks for the stuff," I said. "Was there something else you wanted?" My tone was icy, and he straightened, the smile fading from his lips. He ran a hand through his hair and crossed his arms, glancing around the small yard space and over to Cassie's shop.

"Do you mind if I come in?" He almost seemed nervous about Cassie seeing him. I was tempted to let him stand out in the sun and sweat, both mentally and physically, but I was never one for torture. I swung the door wide and, despite my anger at the man, a little shiver ran down my back as he passed close. Cocoa followed him in and I closed the door on the heat.

"I wanted to say I was sorry again. And I wanted to check on you. I know you're mad at me and I understand. But I want you to know that I truly felt like I had no other option as far as how things happened yesterday. I did it to protect you, but also because it's my job. There was no other option, but I am so sorry that it came at such a cost to you."

I shrugged. I wanted to stay mad at him, but I knew deep down inside that he was speaking the truth. "Okay. I get it. I'm not going to say I forgive you, necessarily. Not right now. But I understand."

His grin lit me up inside and, despite my best intentions, I grinned back.

He bent to pet Cocoa, who once again sprawled out before him. "I also wanted to let you know that all the food from the funeral came back clean. I know it isn't a surprise to you, but I wanted to let you know for sure. We did find traces of poison on a glass of gin, though. It matched the poison that was used on both men. So you were right, someone poisoned his drink."

"Do you know what kind of poison it was?"

He hesitated and then stood up and stuck his hands in his pockets. "They detected high levels of digitoxin in Weiss. The same thing in Roblais, but not enough to kill him."

"Digitoxin. I'm not familiar with that."

"It's a drug that is used as medicine sometimes but too much of it causes nausea, vomiting, and eventually a heart attack, which is what happened to Weiss."

"Were you able to talk to everyone who was there? Did anybody stand out to you?"

He smiled. "I was busy talking to you. But Ty and a couple of the deputies talked to almost everyone. We don't have any major leads yet, but we're working on it. Any more questions, Nancy Drew?"

I huffed. "Good grief, Ryan! I'm just trying to put things together!"

He laughed and put his hands up. "And I'm just trying to lighten the mood. I know you and Cassie love to solve crimes, but please promise me you won't get involved in this, Abby. Please trust that I know what I'm doing. We are working as hard as we can on this. You've got to trust me."

I bit my lip. There was absolutely no way I was going to promise anything of the sort.

Before I responded, the door swung open and Cassie came bouncing inside, halting as soon as she saw Ryan.

"What are you doing here?"

He looked terrified. Which was probably the right response to being on Cassie's bad side.

"I was just leaving," he said. He stooped to give Cocoa one last quick pet and then hightailed it out the door.

"Good riddance," Cassie said with a frown. "What'd he want?"

I told her about the apology but conveniently left out that I'd more or less accepted it. I distracted her with the digitoxin information before she asked too many relationship related questions.

Her eyes widened. "That's more than Ty told me at lunch. The man was a closed book! So frustrating! I wish he wouldn't suck up to Ryan so much. He would tell me more if he didn't think he was gonna get into trouble," she said and blew out a frustrated breath. "We need to look this up," she finished.

I pulled out my laptop and handed it over to her while I went back to the kitchen to continue working on dinner.

Cassie opened the laptop, her fingers flying over the keys as she searched for information. After a few minutes, she leaned in. "Okay, here's what it says about digitoxin. Digitoxin is a cardiac glycoside. It's derived from foxglove plants. In small doses, it's used as a heart medication. But in larger amounts, it can be lethal."

"Foxglove? Isn't that a common garden plant?" I asked her as I pulled my garlic parmesan quick bread out of the oven.

"Yeah, it is," Cassie replied. "It's pretty. I've seen it before. Lots of tall spikes of colorful flowers. But every part of the plant is poisonous. It says here that symptoms of digitoxin poisoning include nausea, confusion, blurred vision, and changes in heart rate. In severe cases, it can cause a heart attack, which fits what happened to Weiss."

Cassie scrolled through the page. "To make it into a poison, someone would need to extract the digitoxin from the plant. It's not something that happens by accident. You need specific knowledge to do it."

I stirred the soup and considered this new information. "So, we're looking for someone who knew enough about foxglove to use it as a poison. That narrows down our list of suspects."

"Exactly," Cassie said, closing the laptop. "And since they found it in his glass, whoever it was must have slipped it into his drink during the event."

I nodded, remembering all the plants at the Weiss house. There were plants everywhere. The backyard was a jungle of green. Who knew what could be growing back there? More and more, Brenda Weiss looked guilty to me. And it wasn't just because I was angry with her for fingering me.

I told Cassie about Brenda's plants and her eyes widened. "Oh, my gosh. That sounds very suspicious. I bet it was her. It's all adding up. How she asked you to cater and then blamed you for the poisoning. It was very convenient. And she no doubt had a hundred and one reasons to want Weiss dead."

"Yeah, but what about Roblais? Ellie said they met once at her bakery, but that doesn't mean there's anything between them."

"What if they were having an affair?" Cassie's eyes widened.

I stuck a spoon into the soup, then blew on the broth and tried it. Nearly perfect. Adding a pinch of salt and one more shake of Italian seasoning, I said, "I don't know. I guess that could be. But that's not what it looked like when they were fighting at the funeral."

"Lover's quarrel?"

I frowned and shrugged. "Maybe." But something about that explanation didn't feel right. "I feel like we're missing something. I don't think we have enough information one way or the other to decide if it was Brenda. For now, I think we should keep digging. The other council members are still on my list. Any of them could have done it, as long as they were also at the funeral."

I shrugged and ladled out the soup for us both, then sliced two thick slabs of bread and buttered them.

"You're right. But my gut says it was Brenda." She closed the laptop and moved into the kitchen to get her bowl. "Thanks for this. It looks delicious!"

I smiled. "I'm happy to, especially after everything you've done for me lately. I have a lot to repay you for."

She waved the comment away. "Come on, we're lifetime pals. It's all water under the bridge."

As we settled into our dinner, Cocoa positioned himself between the two of us, his head resting on one of my feet. Beggar.

"You know what would be helpful? If we could actually talk to Roblais. Maybe we could just ask him about everything? Do you think he's still in the hospital?"

Cassie nodded. "Ty told me they'd questioned him this morning and that he still looked bad."

She got a funny look on her face, and I squinted at her. "What are you thinking over there?"

She smiled, a sly smile. "Maybe nothing. I'll tell you tomorrow."

I could have pressed for more, but I let it drop. We'd had

enough sleuth-talk for one night. And although we didn't have an answer to the question of who killed Weiss, I felt like we'd made serious progress. Now I needed to shift and try to make headway on the party for Saturday. I only hoped we would get a few more reservations, so all the work was worth it.

# Chapter Twenty-Three

The next morning we were hanging out in our pajamas in Cassie's apartment after breakfast, she reading through estate sale listings and I working on a possible new recipe, when Cassie's phone dinged. She read her text and a second later, squealed. "Eek! Guess what?"

I cocked an eyebrow. "Willie Nelson is coming to town?"

"No. Babs McGuire is going to get us in to see Roblais at the hospital. She's a nurse over in the ICU. But we need to go now, before the doctor comes on duty for the day."

I looked around the kitchen where I'd spread a mountain of prep food and sighed. "Is there ever a thing we can do where it doesn't have to be this very minute?"

Cassie grinned. "Not likely."

I threw food into containers and put on some real clothes while Cassie changed and took Cocoa for a quick bathroom break. We met at Cassie's truck five minutes later and zipped through a mostly sleepy Sunday morning Sugar Creek to the small hospital near the freeway where everyone in town went for medical care both large and small. Parking in the nearly empty lot, we hurried inside past the volunteer greeter, who eyed us warily, to the ICU lounge.

Babs McGuire greeted us at the door to the wing. She looked very different all decked out in nurse's attire than she had at the bowling alley a few nights before. Her curly mop of dark hair was tamed back in a tight bun, and her face was clear of the heavy makeup she'd been wearing the last time I saw her. Her blue scrubs swished as we followed her down the hospital corridor. Sugar Creek Hospital was a small affair, and I was nervous about someone seeing and stopping us, but Babs didn't seem to mind at all.

"Thanks, Babs," Cassie said as we tried to keep up.

Babs nodded. "Just don't do anything to get me into trouble, alright? Nothing to get him too excited. He's at risk of a heart attack right now. Don't want to send him over the edge."

We both nodded solemnly. Being accused of killing someone was bad enough. The last thing either of us wanted to do was *actually* kill someone.

She opened the door to a room and motioned for us to follow her in. We crept in behind her as she checked the monitor and made a few notes on a chart. Then she eyed us and nodded. "Five minutes, no more," she whispered as she left the room.

Machines beeped, and the tiny space smelled like antiseptic. Roblais laid in his bed with a mop of greasy hair stuck to his head and a scowl on his face, surfing through the tv that was mounted on the wall. He glanced at us and then back at the tv.

"They won't let me have my phone. Almost had a heart attack when I checked my email yesterday, and they said it was too dangerous. You know what's dangerous? Not checking my email! Who knows what's blowing up without me? It's like a prison over here." The beeping machines at his side picked up in pace and I wondered if we were triggering a heart attack just being in the room. He glanced away from the tv at us again and frowned deeper. "Who are you two? What do you want?"

"Mr. Roblais, I'm Abby Hirsch. I was the one who catered the funeral the other day, where you were poisoned."

The machine picked up the pace again, and I bit my lip. "I didn't poison you, I promise! I'm just here to ask you a few questions because we're trying to figure out who *did* poison you."

"I already talked to the cops."

I nodded. "I know. But we're trying to figure it out too."

"Let me guess, you have a true crime podcast." He rolled his eyes.

"No. Nothing like that. But I'm being framed for the poisonings and I want to clear my name. If you're willing to help, I think we might be able to find the person who poisoned you and Weiss."

He muted the tv and crossed his arms over his chest. He stared at us a full, uncomfortable minute before he finally spoke. "Okay. What do you want to know?"

Cassie and I glanced at each other with fear. Boy, we should have planned this more on the way over. I had no idea what to say.

"We were wondering if you had any ideas about who poisoned you?" Cassie said after a minute.

He looked at her for another long while, so long that I wasn't even sure he would answer. Finally, he shrugged. "A lot of people in this town don't like me, as you probably know already. Don't like the bill I'm trying to get passed."

"We know you supported Weiss when he ran for office in the hopes he would help you pass the bill. Were things not going the way you expected them to go?"

He shrugged. "There's always drama in these small towns. I had a feeling it wouldn't be easy with Weiss. But he was the one who was most willing during the primaries. At least he was willing when it came to taking my money for his campaign. But then he changed his mind when it actually came time to vote. Luckily there were a few others I'd managed to turn after Weiss backed down."

"Who else?"

"Landers was the main one. As soon as I heard he was trying to move away from Sugar Creek, I figured he could be persuaded."

I raised my eyebrows. "I thought Landers was against the bill. I thought that's why he and Weiss got into a fight."

"They got into a fight over the bill, but Landers was backing it and trying to talk sense into Weiss. Without luck, though. Boy, that codger could really dig his heels in when he wanted to. And the kicker is, he was only doing it out of spite for me. Weiss didn't care one bit about the town or the bill." He blew out a frustrated breath. "What a waste that man was. No sense in his head. It doesn't matter though. I'll win eventually."

This was interesting information. The whole time, I'd thought Landers was the one against the bill and Weiss was the one for it. I wondered what it meant for our investigation. I would have to puzzle it out with Cassie later.

"What about Brenda Weiss? I saw you two fighting at the funeral. Do you think she poisoned you?"

He shrugged. "Who knows, that woman is as crazy as her husband was. Small towns," he said with another shake of his head. "I should know better."

"What were you and Brenda fighting about, if you don't mind me asking?"

"I was trying to convince her to take her husband's seat on the council and vote for the bill. But she wasn't having it. Accused me of poisoning her husband, at which point I decided I'd had enough. It was just after we talked that I started feeling sick." His face turned sour as the memory took hold.

At that moment, Babs tapped on the door and opened it. She stuck her head in. "Time's up!" She whispered.

"Thanks, Mr. Roblais," I told him as Cassie and I moved to leave. "Hope you feel better soon." *So you can leave our small town alone.*

He didn't say anything, but turned the tv back on, louder than it had been when we'd come in. Just before I walked out of the room, however, I turned back. "What about the Larsons?"

"The Larsons? What about them?"

"Do you know them? The neighbors?"

He shrugged and cocked an eyebrow. "I know Chad."

"How do you know him? Does he have anything to do with the council or the bill?"

He shook his head. "Nah, just know him from around, I guess."

I frowned. "Okay, thanks." He ignored me and turned back to channel flipping.

We left the room just as the doctor came down the hall and Cassie and I sped through the corridors trying to avoid him. I thought about everything Roblais had said. It was interesting that Brenda Weiss had accused him of poisoning her husband. What would be the point of doing that if *she'd* poisoned her husband? Maybe to make Roblais think it wasn't her?

It was strange, and it made me nervous. Instead of helping out, talking to Roblais had confused me even more.

The greeter gave us the stink-eye again as we cut it through the lobby and out to the parking lot. We both laughed as we booked it to the car, happy to have gotten in and out of the hospital without too much trouble. Mission accomplished.

# Chapter Twenty-Four

After we left the hospital, Cassie and I drove through the still-quiet streets for a few minutes, trying to decide what to do next. She'd called in a teenage part-timer to watch the shop for the day so we could do some estate sale shopping together—her for her shop and me for my catering business—but we'd skipped breakfast in our frenzy to visit Roblais.

"Kolaches?" Cassie asked, taking a right onto the highway before I'd even answered.

I grinned. "Perfect."

Ten minutes later we pulled into the parking lot of the kolache and taco shop off the highway to the south of town and were sitting in the shade eating breakfast as we talked through everything we'd learned.

"The craziest thing to me is that Landers was actually fighting *for* the bill and that he was working with Roblais. All this time, I thought it was the opposite. It doesn't make much sense, if it's true, that he would poison Roblais, right? I mean, I could see him knocking off Weiss, but why try to kill someone who was on his side?"

"We only have Roblais's word to go on. That could be a lie," Cassie replied, as she stretched her legs out in the sun.

"Why lie, though? I don't know. I feel a lot less interested in Landers as the suspect here than I did earlier."

Cassie nodded. "What about Brenda? Did you get a sense one way or another on her? Because, to me, he seemed a little hesitant to talk about her. I wonder if there's more there than he's letting on."

I frowned as I finished my kolache. "Hard to say. She's still top on my list because everything is pointing to her right now. But I'm not sure who else is on that list with her." I felt frustrated by it all. For all the sleuthing we'd done, I felt like we were almost back to zero. "Did you hear what Roblais said on the way out about knowing Chad Larson?"

"Yeah. But is that important? I mean, the Larsons don't seem very connected here, other than their fight over the property line with Weiss. That seems like a pretty silly reason to kill someone. And even if they do know each other, what reason would he have to kill Roblais, too?"

"I'm just saying it's strange that he knows Chad. If Chad doesn't have anything to do with the bill and the lobbyist is only here for the bill, how do they know each other?"

"I don't know. Is it important? I think the stuff he said about Brenda was a lot more interesting."

I didn't have any response because I wasn't sure either. We got back in the truck, both of us quiet with our own thoughts, and headed farther south toward the first of the several estate sales we planned to hit up that day.

I wanted to believe that Brenda was responsible for everything. It was certainly the easiest explanation and it would be satisfying to find out it was really her after she so publicly fingered me as the culprit. But I wasn't convinced yet. The problem was, I didn't know what *would* convince me. Maybe it was pointless for us to even be digging into this. Like last time with Tricia, we were probably causing more harm than good.

I tried to put the thoughts about murder behind me as we pulled up to the first estate sale so I could focus on finding equipment and supplies for my business, but it took a lot of effort. My mind only wanted to work on the poisoning puzzle at hand.

Thankfully, the buzz and joviality of the estate sale scene shifted my thoughts and my mood. The place was a sprawling ranch house, and it was packed floor to ceiling with everything imaginable. I booked it to the kitchen as soon as we entered, and Cassie made a beeline for the furniture.

Over an hour later, I stumbled out to Cassie's truck with my fourth massive box of kitchen goods. It had been a great haul. Not only had I found an entire set of China that would be perfect for the party, I'd snagged a large set of gorgeous antique wine goblets, two cast iron skillets, a massive ceramic mixing bowl, and two boxes of handwritten recipes. I'd always been a sucker for old recipes. I couldn't wait to pour over the yellowed cards and pages inside the boxes.

"Woo, we did good today," Cassie said, grinning, as she stuffed a second gold velvet armchair into the back of her truck bed next to the first. Between the two of us, we'd filled the truck up completely, and this was only the first of three sales we'd planned to visit for the day.

"I guess we should take all this back home before we go anywhere else. You still want to do another one?"

The estate sale had been like a treasure hunt. I'd never been before, but I was hooked now that I knew what to expect, no doubt about it. "Definitely. It'll be good to let Cocoa out for a bit, too."

We chatted about our finds as we headed back to town. I was excited to get everything I bought organized, excited I'd found so much for my business at prices that worked well for my nearly empty wallet.

"You know what we should do?" Cassie said as she finally turned off the freeway toward Sugar Creek half an hour later.

For some reason, I had the feeling I wasn't going to like the answer. "What?"

"We should go over to Brenda's house some night and see if she has foxglove in that jungle of hers."

"Oh, jeez. That is not a good idea. Not at all. We could get arrested. Or shot." But it would certainly help to figure out if Brenda was the primary suspect. I doubted Ryan and Ty had bothered to check on Brenda Weiss's gardening hobby, at least not yet. They might not even know about her obsession with plants. If Brenda had foxglove in her yard, which was used to make the poison that killed her husband and poisoned Weiss, I would probably be convinced that she was guilty. It would be too much of a coincidence.

"I'm just saying. It would clear things up for us a heck of a lot."

"I don't know. It seems really risky. We could mention it to Ryan and Ty and see if they want to go over and look into it."

"You know they'd have to get a warrant to do that. Who knows how long that would take?"

I frowned and looked out the window. Why couldn't things be simple every now and then? And why did Cassie always come up with these crazy harebrained yet impossibly tempting ideas?

"I'll think about it. But right now, I need to focus on this party. I have less than a week and I want it to be really amazing, so word spreads and we can do more in the future."

"Sure, of course. It can wait, I guess. Parties are important. Killers are important too, but yeah. Let's focus on the party."

"Good grief, Cassie. Fine. But not until after the party, alright?"

She didn't answer, but grinned as we pulled around back to her bungalow. I already regretted saying it, but I knew it was too late to back out now. Sleuthing just might be the death of me.

# Chapter Twenty-Five

By Tuesday, Cassie and I had no other leads as far as the murder, but Aunt Meg *had* received four new reservations, almost filling the party up to our goal of twenty. I was happy I'd made the effort to go out to the wineries over the weekend. It seemed to have worked some magic for my business and I made a few notes about the places I'd visited and the owners and employees I'd met so I could keep the relationships up for the future. Who knew what kind of business might come over time? Visions of weddings and anniversary parties and bachelorette parties danced in my head.

It was a tremendous relief, having the reservations, and I threw myself into plans for the dinner. Most of the supplies I'd scavenged over the weekend were already at Primrose House, but I spent the rest of the morning moving things over with Cassie's truck and sorting it all out.

After my third trip of listening to Cocoa's relentless barks, I finally gave in and brought him with me to visit Aunt Meg. He hopped up in the front seat like he owned it and I rolled the window down and let him bark at every car that passed us.

When we arrived, we found Primrose House nearly full of

guests for a girls' trip so I tried to stay out of the way as much as I could, moving in and out the side kitchen door with the dog at my heels.

After finally cramming all my supplies into a side closet we'd designated as makeshift catering space, I brewed myself a cup of earl grey and sat at the kitchen table, Cocoa tucked quietly under my feet. The house was finally quiet because Aunt Meg had accompanied the women on a local shopping trip and I took advantage of the stillness to sit and process. I had a massive amount of planning to do. Making lists for food I needed to buy, I calculated quantities and started a brief timeline for the work leading up to the event that I was sure to change five times before the day. I made a call to hire a temporary helper to serve. As much as I was happy to use local teenagers for most jobs, this dinner was a fancy one and I wanted an experienced server. Not to mention, I wasn't sure how the people of Sugar Creek would feel about me hiring their children, seeing as I was accused of poisoning two people, and I didn't want to put anyone on the spot. I made a mental note to remember Jenny Abernathy's daughter after all the poisoning shenanigans had passed, though.

Maria came in midday after finishing her B&B chores. She pet Cocoa, who lunged for her as soon as she walked in, and then poured herself a glass of ice water from the fridge.

"I'm here until three and ready to help. Your aunt already told me I could, if you needed it."

I smiled. "That would be great. I was hoping we could set tables up outside today, get a feel for the layout now, before we're overwhelmed by kitchen work."

Thirty minutes later, Maria and I pushed the long wood tables I'd borrowed from the Connolys into place under the shade of the live oaks in the yard and stood back to look everything over. I was dripping with sweat, and suddenly I realized we were going to have a big problem that I hadn't even considered. Blame it on too much time in L.A.

"It's way too hot out here," I told Maria. "People aren't going to wanna sit for a long, fancy dinner when they're too hot. They aren't going to want to eat when they're hot."

I put my hands on my hips and frowned, glancing around trying to figure out what we might do about the problem.

"We could try to fit the tables inside," Maria said, but I shook my head.

"There's no way we'd be able to fit so many people inside." Looking around the yard, I noticed Cocoa staring at me with his tongue out. He'd dug himself a small hole in the mud under a tree and seemed to be content to lie there all day.

"I wonder if we could get fans out here," I said, as I paced. "Those massive ones like they have in airplane hangers and industrial style restaurants."

Maria nodded. "That's a good idea," she said. "I've seen some of the wineries do the same thing."

I pulled out my phone and shopped online, wondering how fast we could get something like that delivered or where I would even find fans that would work for what we needed them for.

Of course, the internet came through for me. A few minutes later, I found just the thing and they would supposedly be delivered by Friday. The price was steep, but I knew the fans would come in handy for more than just this event. If we planned to do any more meals here outside in the future, or events like weddings, we would need those fans. I went ahead and ordered them, feeling a grumble in my stomach as I thought about how much money they cost. But with every seat at the dinner nearly taken, I justified the expense. We should be able to make the money up, but it didn't leave much wiggle room for the near future.

*Building a business*, I silently consoled myself. I didn't have my own place to live in, but I was building a business that, with any luck, might just last a lifetime.

Aunt Meg came out the side door a few minutes later as we stood in the shade admiring our work.

"Wow, look at this! I had no idea this place could look so good!"

I told her about the fans, and she nodded. "Investing in your business is a good idea. I know it hurts up front, but I really think we're going to be successful. I just got the final reservation for Saturday."

We all did a little happy dance, and then Aunt Meg turned a critical eye to our work. "We could use a little more decor though, don't you think?"

I nodded, but as Aunt Meg motioned for us to follow her back to a large shed that sat at the back of the property, Maria told us it was time for her to leave for the day. We thanked her for her work, and said goodbye. Then Aunt Meg and I moved over to the shed.

"Let's see what we can find. I haven't looked through this stuff since Christmas, other than storing a few things from the wedding," she told me as she pulled out a key and inserted it into a padlock door. The rusty hinge creaked open, and I flinched as I heard a scurry inside.

We looked at each other wildly. "You got a broom or a shovel or something?" I asked her. "Who knows what that is!"

Aunt Meg reached around inside and found a broom and a mop. Handing one to me, she took the other one for herself. "It's probably just a raccoon or a mouse," she said.

At least it wasn't likely that it was a snake. Snakes didn't make that kind of racket. Nothing, in my opinion, would be as bad as finding a snake.

We went inside slowly, both of us ready to hit at whatever came at us. The shed was dim and dusty, and it was hard to see much of anything at all except stacks of boxes and tools. Another shuffling noise came from the corner, and despite my best efforts and keeping a level ahead, I yelped and tossed my broom around wildly.

Aunt Meg laughed at me and moved toward the noise. She'd always been braver than I had. She poked around behind a box until at last a tiny possum came darting out at us, making me jump in the air and throw the broom. I was useless in the face of small creatures. Absolutely useless.

The poor thing was able to make it out of the shed without taking any damage from us, although I'd bet my dinner that he was as scared as I was.

"Hopefully, that's the last of that," Aunt Meg said as she started to sort through boxes. I picked my broom back up, not ready to be unarmed, and watched her. "A lot of this is Christmas stuff, but I did save some of the things from the wedding, the lights and the candles and whatnot. Might come in handy for Saturday. I might have a few things too from those Easter parties we used to do."

I remembered the massive Easter egg hunts that she and my Uncle Nolan used to host every year when my brother and I were kids. It brought back fond memories.

"I bet you've got all kinds of things we could use in here," I said.

"No doubt, with your creativity. I'm sure we can find all kinds of things. And if this dinner party thing becomes a regular event for us, we're going to need it all."

We started going through boxes and I put aside anything that seemed like it might be useful. Very soon, we had a stack of things for the party. After a while, we took it all inside and dusted and organized it into piles. It was dirty work, and I grinned when Aunt Meg went to the fridge and pulled a pitcher of tea with lemon slices out of the fridge.

She poured us both the glass and handed me one. "This is pretty good work," she said as she surveyed the yard from the picture window over the sink. "I think people are really going to like it. With any luck, they'll tell their friends."

I moved over to gaze out at the yard too and wrapped an arm around her thin shoulders. With all that had happened between the festival and the funeral, the death and the poisoning, I'd nearly forgotten why I'd come back to Sugar Creek. But here she was, standing right next to me. I hugged her into me, feeling nostalgic and a little teary.

"It's all going to work out, you'll see," I told her, happy to be on the other side of the crippling anxiety and depression that had plagued me since the upsetting funeral events. The distraction of physical labor and the elation of filling up our reservations had worked wonders on my mood.

She hugged me back and after another minute we said goodbye for the day and I collected Cocoa and went out to the truck. It was time to get home and take a much needed shower. I was absolutely exhausted by the end of the day, but I felt really confident too. If nothing else, this dinner would be beautiful. Between the luxury hilly landscape of Primrose House, the twinkling candlelight and flower arrangements, and the vintage dishes I'd found with Cassie, the night would be lovely.

Now I just needed to make the food magic happen.

# Chapter Twenty-Six

Friday morning dawned hot and humid. I pulled on shorts and a t-shirt, then moisturized and brushed out my hair. Declaring myself ready for anything, I slipped on a pair of flip-flops and leashed up Cocoa for his morning romp through Cassie's neighborhood.

It would be a busy day. I ran through my list of chores for the party, trying to calm the nervousness brewing. My time in the catering industry had never been so fraught with anxiety, although I hadn't been the one in charge of anything back in L.A., so that wasn't much of a surprise. The wedding in April had given me a small taste of the stress that ownership entailed, but I was starting to wonder if I'd signed up for a life of high anxiety with this business, or if I might eventually get used to it all and these events would feel as old hat as working in L.A. had felt.

There was a lot more on the line this time around, too. Aunt Meg was relying on me to bring in more business. She would never say it, but I knew it was true. The B&B needed more guests. There was no way around it. And I'd banked my entire life on this all working out. So the stakes were high. A lot higher than I was comfortable with. But I was just going to have to push through it. And keep antacids in my pocket.

After getting Cocoa settled, I headed downtown to the store in the Connolys van, which I'd borrowed once again, with a list as long as my arm. I really needed to work on getting myself a catering truck. But that was something I didn't have the money for yet. Maybe after another couple of good gigs, it would happen.

I hoped the shopping wouldn't take more than a couple of hours because I had an immense pile of prep work to get done before the sun set. Besides going to the local H.E.B. for all the staples, I would need to stop by Henderson's Fine Foods for the proteins I'd ordered. Tomorrow was the big event, so there wasn't a lot of wiggle room left.

Downtown was the usual mix of kids on summer break, tourists strolling Main Street, and locals doing errands. On a sudden hunch, I turned right and headed toward Town Hall for a quick detour. I parked and walked inside, hoping to find Gina still in charge of the permit office.

Sure enough, she was at the front desk and greeted me with a smile.

"Hey, it's my favorite caterer! How are you, Abby? Need another business license?" She laughed, and I laughed too. I liked Gina. She was good people.

"No, no, nothing like that. I was wondering if you might be able to tell me a couple of things."

Her face grew serious. "Sure, Abby. What is it?"

"At Andy Weiss's funeral the other day, Chad Larson was talking about some property line dispute he had with the Weiss family. I wondered if you knew anything about that."

She nodded and rolled her eyes. "If only I didn't. It was a regular thorn in our side over here. Larson claimed that the property assessment he received when he bought his property showed the property line being a full six feet further over toward the Weiss house. He claimed that their fence was on his property and he wanted to take it down and move it over. But of course, Weiss was in charge here, so nothing ever happened. I don't know what claim Weiss had to ignore the request, other than it was his own property. He wouldn't let anyone else in the office see the documents. Big surprise, I know. The Larsons even got a fancy lawyer a few months back, and they were pursuing a suit against him, but I don't know how far that got."

"Has Larson been in since Weiss died to try again?"

"No. Which is kind of funny. I would've thought he'd get here faster than a sneeze through a screen door to get that problem taken care of, now that Weiss is no longer with us." She looked puzzled.

I frowned. "Huh. Strange. Well, that's all I was wondering about. Thanks for the info. I hope you have a good weekend!"

"You too, honey! Nice to see you again. Drop in any time!"

I turned her words over and over in my mind as I shopped for supplies ten minutes later. It didn't seem to make sense. I could have sworn that Chad Larson was yelling about how he would be at the permit office on Monday morning to take care of the property dispute. Hadn't that been what had set Brenda off, that had led the Larsons to leave the funeral party, and to find Roblais outside?

For the first time, I thought about how easily we could have all stayed inside that day as he struggled and died in front. Roblais was supremely lucky that the Larsons had left the funeral when they had. A few minutes later, and he may have died.

I couldn't make heads or tails of why the Larsons would be sitting on the property line issue. There wasn't anything else I could do about it at the moment, though, so I turned my focus to the task at hand. Luckily, I found the store largely empty as I parked. Everyone must have been out enjoying the summer.

A few minutes later, I grabbed a cart and started making my way through the aisles. I tried to stay organized as I went, but the more I put in the cart, the more difficult it became. My list was like a war-zone and my cart was filling fast.

I was nearly done with the shopping when I turned onto the baking aisle and ran right into Patty Larson, who had a shaker of lemon pepper in her hand.

"Oh! Good morning!" she said, putting the seasoning back on the shelf and turning to me with a smile. "You're Abby, right? The caterer?"

She stuck out her hand, and I smiled and took it, happy she didn't seem to be in the thinking-I-was-a-murderer camp. "Yep. And you're Patty? Sorry we didn't get a chance to meet earlier."

"The festival was very busy. And upsetting." Her face turned down, and I frowned and nodded.

"I heard that you're usually the one to win the Peachy Keen competition. You must have been upset that it got closed down, too."

She nodded. "It was very sad. I work all year on my recipes, and this year I had especially good ones. Although from what I hear, you might have beat me, anyway." She gave me a friendly smile. "Peachy Keen isn't the only competition I participate in. I run the competition circuit all through Texas. Ribs, chili, cornbread... you name it. If there's a cooking competition, I enter."

"Wow, I didn't realize that there were so many competitions out there."

"It keeps me very busy. And I really enjoy cooking. Now that my kids are gone I don't have that many people to cook for, so the competitions give me a reason to keep trying new things, improving. You know," she said with a shrug.

I nodded and smiled. I could spot another foodie a mile away. I knew that Patty was a woman after my own heart.

"We should get together sometime, exchange recipes. I'd love to know more about the competitions around here," I told her.

She beamed at me. "That would be wonderful. I don't have a lot of friends in Sugar Creek. At least not people who are as interested in cooking as I am. My husband certainly doesn't care," she said with a small shrug.

I frowned, trying to figure her out. But she seemed genuine and friendly enough and I exchanged phone numbers with her so we could find a time to meet. She seemed very nice, and I realized that in my mind I'd equated her with her husband, and had assumed that she was mean and ugly, just like him. But maybe I'd been wrong to judge her so harshly. She seemed like a good person to get to know. After another minute of chit-chat about cooking, I glanced at my watch and my heart skipped a beat.

"Well, I should probably get going. I've got a thing tomorrow, got a lot to do..."

Her eyes brightened. "Oh! I heard about that party you're putting on! What a good idea! I wish I could have gotten a seat. Maybe next time? Good luck with it."

I smiled. "Thanks, I'll need it. Let's talk soon, okay?"

"Yes, definitely. I'm so glad we ran into each other today."

"Same here. Have a good weekend!"

We went our separate ways, and I finished up the rest of my shopping quickly. Our conversation had slowed me down, but I was glad for it. Who knew? Maybe I'd just made a new friend.

# Chapter Twenty-Seven

When I got back to the B&B, I booked it into the kitchen with the first of many bags of groceries. I was happy to find both Maria and Aunt Meg waiting for me. Between the three of us, we made quick work of unloading the van.

"I need to get a wagon or something, I think," I told them with a laugh. I must hav been logging a lot of steps back and forth from the parking lot to the kitchen. At least I was getting some exercise. The kitchen was a disaster, however, and it took a good half an hour before we'd organized and put all the food away as best we could. The key to everything was organization, so even though it took precious time, I knew it was a worthwhile activity.

Finally, I pulled my apron on and started peeling carrots as Maria chopped parsley and chives for the green goddess dressing and Aunt Meg got to work slicing the big loaves of bread I'd bought into cubes. As we worked, I told them about what I'd found out from Gina and about running into Patty Larson.

"It's strange that they haven't done anything about the property issue yet, given how much of a stink they made at the funeral party the other day," I said.

"That *is* odd," Aunt Meg replied. "How did they react to Roblais being poisoned? Maybe that spooked them?"

I shrugged. "They left pretty quick. I didn't even see them again after I called 9-1-1. Although I wasn't exactly paying attention."

"It's a good point about Patty wanting to win the competition," Maria said. "She wouldn't have done anything to mess that up, it seems to me."

I nodded as I roughly chopped the carrots and added them to a massive stock pot with chunks of fresh ginger and vegetable stock. I would slowly simmer the mixture until everything was tender, add in some fresh herbs and butter, and use an immersion blender to turn it into a deliciously smooth soup. Once it chilled overnight, the ginger would mellow out and meld with the snap of the carrots. I knew that a bowl of the cold soup would be a welcome treat to diners sitting outside tomorrow, and would get the party off to a deliciously refreshing start.

"Patty was so nice today," I said, turning my attention to washing and prepping tender baby spinach, kale, and arugula. I wanted the salad components all ready to go so I could toss it at the last minute just before serving. "We exchanged numbers so we can talk food sometime. You're right, Maria. I have a hard time imagining her involved in any of this. Her husband seems like a troublemaker, though, from what little I've seen of him."

"I don't know the family well. They've been in town a long time, but our paths never really crossed," Aunt Meg said.

After I finished with the greens, I stretched my neck and surveyed all we'd accomplished. We were making good progress, but there was still plenty to finish.

"Alright, I need to stop here for a while and go pick up the meats from Georgie. I think I've got it from here on out for today, although I want us all to start bright and early tomorrow, if that works."

"Woo!" Aunt Meg said, and wiped her brow. "We did good, girls. This party is going to be amazing!"

I nodded and grabbed a bottled water. "It sure is!" And I meant it. Things were definitely looking up. After I put a few things away and said goodbye, I headed back out to the Connolys van to go shopping once more. The life of a caterer was a life of shopping.

Right as I pulled into a parking spot along Main Street, Cassie called and I answered.

"Hey, what's up?" I said.

"Abby! You will not believe what I just heard from Ty!"

"What?"

"The F.B.I. was called in. They're with Roblais now."

My eyes widened. "Are you kidding me?"

"No! Ty said someone called in a tip to Ryan this morning about campaign fraud or bribery or something, and he had to get the F.B.I. involved. They're over at the hospital questioning him. Ryan's with them, but Ty said they're taking over the poisoning cases, too. They think it's all connected."

"No way. This is big news, Cassie!" I leaned back in my seat, trying to wrap my head around it all and failing miserably.

"Does this mean they know who murdered Weiss?" I asked.

"I don't know. Probably won't know much until Ryan gets back to the station. Ty didn't really know what was going on, either. I guess we'll have to wait to see."

"Okay, keep me posted. I'm smack dab in the middle of all this catering stuff, but I'll keep my phone on me."

We hung up, and I hopped out of the van, my mind spinning with new information as I made my way into Henderson's Fine Foods.

The shop was cool and calm, and I took a moment to catch my breath. Between the catering work and the F.B.I. excitement, my heart and mind were racing. Georgie's shop was a cool reprieve from the madness that surrounded me. Stocked with gourmet cheeses, olives, and other delicious and intriguing exports, the shop always got my creative juices flowing.

"Hey, Abby! Glad you're here!" Georgie said as she came around the counter at the front and gave me a quick hug. "I've got the steaks, salmon, and shrimp for you. Boy, you're cooking up a proper feast over at Primrose House, I guess!"

I nodded and followed her back to her walk-in cooler, where she pulled a few boxes for me.

"I'm hoping so! Only twenty reservations this time, but if it works out, we might double it next time. This is just a first run. See how things go."

"Good luck to you, then. Stop by next week and let me know how it goes. I have a special shipment of tinned seafood coming in from Spain on Wednesday I want you to try, too. I think you'll like it."

I grinned and piled the boxes up and headed for the door. She followed me and opened it. "That sounds great, Georgie! Will do!"

I was starting to feel the pressure big time, and I drummed my fingers on the steering wheel as I zipped back through town again. I would have to get the Connolys a special present for letting me use their poor suffering VW van so much lately. I was putting the poor thing through its paces with all the running around.

The rest of the day flew by in prep work and lists. Despite the fever pitch of activity, I kept a close eye on my phone, hoping to hear more from Cassie, but by the time I'd finished at the B&B for the day, her call still hadn't come. I shrugged it off as I cleaned up the kitchen, knowing I'd see her soon enough at home.

When I got back to Cassie's place, I was downright exhausted. I had done everything I'd wanted to get done for the day, though, so I was feeling pretty good about it all. But I was buzzing to know what was going on with the investigation.

"You didn't call me," I said as I walked in and found Cassie pacing. Cocoa jumped off the couch and came at me with his customary enthusiastic greeting. I got on the floor and gave him a proper hello.

"That's because I haven't heard anything. I called Ty twice, but he said Ryan still hadn't come back to the station," she said.

"Boy, talk about a marathon interrogation. They must really be going at it. I'm surprised the hospital is allowing it. They seemed pretty concerned he'd have a heart attack the last time we were there."

"Babs told me they technically discharged him today but that the F.B.I. arrived before he left and they've been there in some extra exam room ever since."

I raised my eyebrows. "Well, at least they're working on it." I rolled my shoulders, aching for a shower and a good night's sleep. "I've got to get to bed. Tomorrow's going to be a bear."

"Okay. You want me to wake you up if I hear anything?"

"Nah, you can tell me in the morning."

At least now we didn't have to continue to sleuth on our own. I'd really not wanted to go snooping in the Weiss yard and said a silent prayer of thanks as I left Cassie, happy that I could shift my focus more completely onto the catering side of my life now that the F.B.I. had taken over. Because come tomorrow, I would need all the focus I could get.

# Chapter Twenty-Eight

The next morning, soft light filtered in through the curtains, nudging me awake. The day's big event hung over me like a cloud of both excitement and pressure. I swung my legs out of bed and quickly dressed in jeans and a t-shirt. As I tied my hair back and slipped into my sturdy kitchen clogs, a sense of purpose settled over me. This was it, the day I'd been preparing for. If it worked out, we could be certain of more like it. If it worked out, it might mean more guests for the B&B. But if it didn't work out, I wasn't sure what it meant. That wasn't really a possibility, though, I reminded myself. I'd planned and prepared this event to within an inch of its life, and I knew deep down that I could run it in my sleep.

Ready for the day's challenges, I gave Cocoa some love before grabbing my keys and heading out, my mind already running through the dishes and preparations awaiting me at the B&B. I'd thought about waking Cassie and asking her if she ever heard from Ty, but I needed to focus on my work, and I knew she needed her sleep. I would find out what happened soon enough, I was sure of it.

Stepping outside, I felt the early morning sun warm against my skin, a stark contrast to the cool air of Cassie's house. On the way over to Primrose House, I stopped at the bakery to pick up the tarts from Ellie. I'd ordered a few extra beyond the twenty that we would need, wanting to be prepared for any last-minute problems, but also knowing it would be a perfect treat for the staff after the party if any were left over.

Peaking into the top box, I grinned. "Wow, Ellie, these are absolutely beautiful! I can't wait to serve them."

"Take some pictures," she told me. I wish I could be there.

"Will do. Have a good day!"

The drive to Primrose House was short, but my mind was miles ahead, planning every detail of the day. Pulling into the B&B's gravel driveway, the sight of the old familiar building greeted me, its windows catching the morning light. It was a beautiful sight. If nothing else, we had a prime location for a party. The fans I ordered had come the night before, which was a load of worry off my mind. It wouldn't be pleasant outside, exactly. But it would be bearable.

Aunt Meg met me in the front lobby, wiping her hands on her apron as she walked toward me. "Good morning, Abby! Ready for the big day?"

I smiled, balancing a box of tarts carefully in my arms. "As ready as I'll ever be. How are things looking here?"

"We're ready to work," Aunt Meg replied, leading the way back to the kitchen. "Maria's already started on some of the prep work."

The three of us snuck another look at the tarts before I stashed them away in the fridge. Each round tart had a beautiful circle of peaches fanned out with a drizzle of honey glaze and sprinkle of cinnamon on top. I would take them out about an hour before the party so they could come to room temperature.

After looking over my notebook for the day, I got to work prepping shrimp as I told Maria and Aunt Meg about the F.B.I. taking over the case. They were both happy to know that something was being done.

"So this means no more sleuthing for you," Aunt Meg said with a smile. Clearly, she was happy to not have to worry about me anymore. At least not in that department.

Before I could answer her, my phone rang. I washed my hands quickly and answered, barely catching Cassie before she went to voicemail.

"Okay, here's what Ty had to report this morning. Sounds like after hours of questioning, the F.B.I. finally took Roblais back to Austin last night. They're charging him with bribery and some sort of corruption charges. And that Sugar Creek Sheriff's office was officially off the murder case because it had to do with Roblais."

"So that's it, then. We just need to let the F.B.I. do its thing?"

"I guess so. Not very satisfying, but that's what's going on. I still think we should keep our eyes and ears out, though. I mean, those guys went back to Austin! How are they going to solve a crime in Sugar Creek?"

"Did Ty say what they questioned him about for all that time?" I stuck the phone between my ear and shoulder and arranged bread cubes on trays to brown in the oven for the panzanella, then stuck them in to broil.

"He didn't want to say, other than it had to do with the council members and bribes."

"So maybe Landers, then," I speculated. I wasn't a bit surprised to know that Roblais had been doing something illegal. I wondered who had turned him in for it, though. And why now, after all this time?

"Okay, thanks for keeping me posted. Things are getting pretty crazy here, but I'll talk to you tonight after I'm done with the party."

I hung up with Cassie and told Maria and Aunt Meg what she'd told me, which felt like not much of anything at the end of the day. Roblais was doing something illegal involving the city council. Big surprise. It still didn't really tell us who had killed Weiss or poisoned Roblais.

As Aunt Meg and I continued our conversation, the smell of something burning suddenly wafted through the air. My eyes widened in realization. "The bread cubes!" I exclaimed, rushing to the oven. Pulling open the door, a cloud of smoke billowed out, setting off the kitchen's smoke alarm.

The sharp, piercing sound of the alarm sent a jolt of panic through me. Aunt Meg hurried over, waving a tea towel to clear the air around the device. Coughing slightly from the smoke, I quickly turned off the oven and grabbed the charred tray, setting it aside. Just as the alarm stopped beeping, the temp worker I'd hired came into the kitchen.

Perfect timing.

"Uh, hi. I'm here for the catering job?" The young woman looked deeply skeptical as she took in the kitchen in utter chaos and the three women trying to put out the fire alarm.

"Great, you're just in time! The first thing I need you to do is run down to the store and pick up three loaves of sourdough bread."

She frowned and then walked back out the door. I hoped she was on her way to H.E.B. rather than on her way home.

"Completely forgot about them," I muttered, my heart racing as I scanned the kitchen and the charred bread remains. Served me right for continuing the ridiculous sleuthing when I should have had my full attention on my kitchen duties.

A few curious guests poked their heads into the kitchen, drawn by the commotion. Aunt Meg, ever the gracious host, quickly reassured them with her usual charm. "Just a little culinary excitement, folks! No need to worry, everything is under control." She left to go calm the worried guests, and Maria and I started to clean up the mess and organize the kitchen all over.

Eventually, the worker came back with the loaves of bread. I quickly chopped them into cubes and threw them back in the oven, keeping a close eye on them as she introduced herself as

Maggie and I filled her in on the party that was due to start in less than an hour.

She fell in line quickly beside us and I was relieved to find her capable and experienced. Exactly what I needed for the party. I sent her out after a few minutes with a bottle of champagne in a bucket of ice and a tray of glasses to get ready for things to begin.

Once the guests arrived, things really kicked into high gear. I stirred and tasted the soup and sauces and kept stealing glances out to the yard in the shade of the evening, hoping to time the steak and fish course just right. It was extremely tricky, especially with a plated dinner like this, but at least all the other components for the evening were finally ready to go.

Men and women took flutes of champagne from Maggie and mingling with one another near the table. The lights twinkled in the trees, and the candles worked their magic between the plates and glasses set out for dinner. It was really beautiful, and I took a moment to appreciate all that we'd accomplished and to say a silent prayer of gratitude that it had all come together.

"All right, honey," Aunt Meg said as she came in the kitchen door a few minutes later, wiping sweat from her brow. "The guests are all here. Do you want me to have them sit down at the table? It's a little hot running around, but those fans sure do help when people are sitting down."

I nodded. It was go time.

"That would be great, and have Maggie pour that first Riesling and then come in for the soup. I'll be out in a minute."

I ran to the guest bathroom for a quick check. My hair was still mostly in its bun and I didn't have any flour on my face. Ready to go.

Maria grabbed my hand and squeezed as I walked by her. "Everything looks so amazing, Abby. And I know all the food is incredible. There's no way this won't lead to more business for you and hopefully for the B&B. I have to go, but good luck tonight."

I gave her a quick hug and a smile. "I couldn't have done it without you. You have some mad kitchen skills. Aunt Meg better be careful. I might try to steal you to work only for me."

She laughed, and I adjusted my chef coat before heading out to talk to the guests.

As the evening sun began to dip below the horizon, casting a golden glow over the B&B's garden, I took a deep breath and stepped out onto the patio. The guests, fanning themselves in the lingering heat, turned their attention toward me.

"Good evening, everyone," I began, my voice carrying over the soft murmur of conversation. "I want to thank you all for joining us tonight, especially in this Texas heat. Your presence here makes all our efforts worthwhile."

Ten minutes later, after I'd introduced myself, talked about the menu, showcased Brandon's hot sauce, and settled everyone with their first course, I stepped back inside and began cooking the protein. I was finally at the point in the evening where the stress began to ease off and it looked like things would work out.

Despite the craziness that had been my life since arriving in Sugar Creek, and despite the chaos that had been the kitchen only a couple of hours before, things were looking up for me and my little catering business. The success with the dinner party helped me to feel like I was finally going in the right direction.

Two hours later, after we cleaned up the surrounding mess, paid Maggie and sent her on her way, and said goodbye to the last dinner guest, Aunt Meg and I took a minute to celebrate with some of the leftover champagne and one of Ellie's peach tarts. Both of us had grins plastered on our faces as we processed what we'd accomplished.

"It was a good day, Abby. You did me proud, honey."

"I couldn't have done it without you. You are so good with people. Much better than I could ever be."

"We make a good team. There's no denying it," she replied.

I snagged another of the tarts to take to Cassie and then hugged her goodnight. "Get some good sleep. We can get together sometime tomorrow to go over everything. But it looks good from a money perspective. Between the cost of the dinner and all the tips people left us, we were firmly in the black for the dinner." It didn't include all the equipment, the fans, and the rest of it. But thinking in easy terms was all I could handle after a solid day's work.

"Sounds good. Sleep well. Love you."

There was a skip to my step as I finally made my way to my car and headed back to Cassie's house. Nothing could get in the way of my good mood. Or my bed.

At least, it seemed that way, until I arrived at Cassie's place.

# Chapter Twenty-Nine

I was exhausted and smelly by the time I finally got back to Cassie's place after catering the party. Unfortunately, Cassie was waiting by the door for me.

"How was it?" she asked, following me around the kitchen as I poured myself a big glass of ice water. Cocoa bounced around too, and I felt like I was under attack. All I wanted was a shower.

"It was good. But exhausting. I brought you one of Ellie's tarts," I told her and put it on the counter.

She leaned over it, her eyes wide. "Ooh, thanks! That looks delicious!"

I sighed. "I might have a bed day tomorrow." Lounging in my pajamas, reading a book, playing with Cocoa. It sounded like a perfect Sunday to me. One that I had absolutely deserved and desperately needed.

"Oh, that sounds nice! So, listen..."

Oh, no. I shook my head, not even wanting to hear it.

"Jan Donovan, who runs the Sugar Creek Planning Committee, was in the shop today and I overheard her say that Brenda Weiss and her son are visiting family in Austin, but that they're coming back tomorrow. This is the perfect time to check out her yard."

"No. No way. The F.B.I. is going to figure this out, remember? The F.B.I. doesn't need us to check anything out."

"You and I both know we can look into this way faster than the F.B.I. with all of their red tape and whatnot. They aren't even in town right now, for crying out loud! Please, Abby. Just this last thing. We can tell Ryan if we find something and then we can be done. I promise."

I continued to shake my head as I guzzled my water. My feet ached, but not as much as my back. There was no way on earth I wanted to go break the law at that moment. What I wanted was to crawl into bed.

"If we don't do this now, we might never get another chance!" Cassie whined.

I walked by her, ignoring her pleas, and headed straight for the shower. I couldn't. I wouldn't.

But as I turned the faucet on, I sighed.

Of course I could. Of course I would.

"You're killing me, Cassie. Give me five," I said through the bathroom door, where I knew she waited on the other side.

She let out a yip and so did Cocoa. I cried a little on the inside as I slipped out of my catering clothes and into a black t-shirt and dark jeans. I was almost too tired to stand, but I knew that Cassie was right. This might be our last chance for a late-night sleuthing session. I doubted anyone in the fancy neighborhood would notice us, but I dressed in my darkest clothes as I wondered if the Weiss residence had cameras. The thought nearly gave me a heart attack. But I figured she had it coming to have me break into her yard after fingering me as a murderer with absolutely no proof.

A few minutes later, we prepared to leave, all geared up with flashlights and the pink gardening gloves that had come in so handy the last time we'd gone on a clandestine snooping mission. I figured it was dark enough out that nobody would notice the glaring color, especially if we waited until we were in the backyard to slip them on.

As we headed out the door, Cocoa ran out between us at the speed of light. He'd never tried to run away before and we called him frantically before we realized that he was headed straight for the car. He wanted to tag along, too.

I wasn't sure it was a good idea. What if we lost him? What if he made a noise and someone saw us? But he would not be convinced to go back inside, no matter how many treats we promised, and after a minute of debate, we decided he might just be an asset. It was a risk, but he'd proved himself to be loyal and helpful before. Why would tonight be any different?

The night air was cooler than I expected as Cassie, Cocoa, and I sped through the dark streets to the Weiss house. Cocoa, perched excitedly in the back seat, seemed as eager as Cassie for the night's adventure. I just hoped our late-night escapade wouldn't end in disaster.

We parked a block away and sat staring a minute into the darkness.

"Should we leave Cocoa here?" I asked, worried that we would get the dog lost or, even worse, hurt.

"I doubt we could if we wanted to."

As soon as we tried leaving the truck, her suspicion was confirmed as he let out a yip.

"He's going to bark so much that we'll be found out," Cassie said.

I shrugged and opened the door for him and he hopped out with purpose, following us with a bounce in his step.

The street was quiet, with only the occasional flicker of a TV screen visible through neighborhood windows. Every crunch of gravel under our feet sounded like a thunderclap in the still night as we headed up the drive to the back of the house.

Cocoa kept pace with us as we snuck up to the back gate of the Weiss property. He seemed to understand the need for stealth, moving quietly at our heels. Cassie and I slipped on our pink gardening gloves, and with a deep breath, we eased the gate open.

The place was an absolute jungle. I'd seen nothing like it before. I moved my pen light back and forth on the tiny path, hoping to avoid stepping on any of the plants, but it was nearly impossible. Vines and shrubs crowded every inch of space. This family took their gardening very seriously.

I wondered again if we should be doing this as we passed below a darkened window. I hated the idea of getting caught. And the couple had seemed so strange, so unhinged. Who could tell how people like that might react to intruders in their yard? And who knew for sure if they were really out of town? We were operating on a big fat assumption fueled by the gossip wheel. I wouldn't be one bit surprised if they had a gun. Most people in Sugar Creek did. It was part of the culture, for better or worse. My heart pounded in my throat as I ran through all the possibilities of how this could go very wrong for us.

Cocoa charged in first, his nose to the ground and tail wagging wildly. We followed cautiously, our flashlights casting long, eerie shadows across the yard.

The backyard was a maze of greenery. Tall shrubs, overgrown vines, and an array of flowers turned the space into a dense mini-forest. We'd both studied pictures of foxglove on the internet before we left Cassie's place, but I wasn't sure I'd be able to find the plant even if it *was* in this yard.

"It's like something out of a fairy tale," Cassie whispered, awe mixed with a hint of apprehension in her voice. "It sure is pretty. Hard to imagine someone with such a tender spot for plants could kill another human."

I shrugged, knowing all too well that people were very often a mystery.

We moved slowly along the narrow path, our lights darting around, half expecting something—or someone—to jump out at us. Cocoa sniffed around with purpose, his movements swift and sure.

As we delved deeper into the garden, the sense of isolation grew. The sounds of the neighborhood faded away, replaced by the rustle of leaves and the occasional night bird. It felt like stepping into another world, one where secrets and mysteries lurked in every shadow.

Then, suddenly, Cocoa stopped. His body tensed, ears perked up, and he started digging furiously under the fence to the house next door.

"Cocoa, no!" I whispered, trying to get to him before he went under the fence. But it was no use. He was just small enough to push his way under a loose board and into the yard next door.

"Shoot!" Cassie said, and we rushed over, shining our lights on the spot where Cocoa was digging in the neighbor's yard. He made quick work of a spot under a bush as we watched. A few minutes later, he rooted around and then pulled something out of the ground.

Cassie and I held our breath as we watched him trot back to the fence with it. But before he got all the way, a light snapped on. Someone came out onto the porch in the yard where Cocoa was. All three of us froze.

"Who's out there?" Chad Larson yelled into the night. As far as I knew, he couldn't see us. He squinted into his yard, scanning for something. And that's when I noticed that he had a gun. My heart froze in my throat and Cassie and I both ducked below the fence where we'd been watching Cocoa.

"I know someone's out there," he yelled. "I'm calling the cops!" His face was twisted in anger, his posture tense. I prayed for our little Cocoa to be careful, prayed that Chad wouldn't see him.

A few seconds later, as we crouched together at the fence line wondering what to do, Cocoa pushed back through the fence, quiet as a mouse. In his mouth was the thing he'd dug up. He dropped it at our feet with a wag of his tail.

Cassie and I peered at it and realized that it was a small glass vial with a rubber stopper, like a medicine bottle. We made faces at each other. Surely this couldn't be the poison bottle. Cocoa had no way of knowing that's what we were after, did he?

My heart pounded in my ears and I forced tears back as we both pet him. I'd been so scared for him, so worried that Chad would see him and shoot him, that I'd almost stopped breathing. Now, I hugged him to me tight and waited in Brenda's bushes for Chad to go back inside so we could get the heck out of dodge.

But that was not to be our fate.

# Chapter Thirty

Before we were able to make our exit from the Weiss yard, the lights of a police cruiser poured over us and we knew the jig was up.

Cocoa was all too happy to give us away when he spotted Ryan at the back gate. The dog ran over, tail wagging, and Ryan sighed, putting his head down a moment before looking over to Chad Larson's yard.

"It's okay, Mr. Larson. I've found them." Ryan waited, watching as Chad went back inside and then motioned to us.

"Come on, you two," he said, disappointment clouding his voice.

We stood and dusted ourselves off and I pulled the gardening gloves off and stuck them in my back pocket. Cocoa trotted along beside him as he led the way to his cruiser parked in the Weiss driveway. If I didn't know any better, I would say that Cocoa liked Ryan even more than he liked us.

A minute later Ryan opened the back door of the cruiser for us. "You two are going to be the death of me, I swear it," he said, as I passed him and slipped inside. The anger radiated off him and he slammed the door after we were both inside, then opened the front passenger door for Cocoa. Good grief.

"I thought you promised to stop sleuthing," he said as he started the ignition.

"Well, I thought you'd have the decency to not arrest me in front of a crowd, but here we are," I snapped back.

"I didn't arrest you, I took you in for questioning."

"Po-tay-toes, Po-tah-toes." He was such a man, jeez. "Who cares what you call it, the outcome is the same. People think I poisoned someone with my food."

"You know I'm gonna have to actually book you two. If Chad presses charges you girls might have a criminal record on your hands. I can't believe that you would do something this ridiculous."

"I don't think Chad is going to press any charges," I told him as I slipped the vial out of my pocket. "Especially not after what we found. Or I should say, what Cocoa found." I glanced at Cassie and she nodded. I held up the vial for Ryan to see.

"What's that?" he asked.

"A vial that Cocoa dug up under Chad Larson's bushes."

He frowned as he looked from us to the vial and back again through the rearview mirror. The three of us sat in the police cruiser, processing everything for a moment, and then Ryan drove us all down to the station. It was the second time I'd left the Weiss residence in police custody. Rather embarrassing. At least this time there wasn't an audience.

We were all quiet on the drive back. Cocoa gazed out the window, and I wondered just how much trouble we were really in. I hoped that the vial was meaningful. I hoped that it had digitoxin inside. But for all I knew it could be full of plant fertilizer. We'd really stepped in it, again.

Ryan's expression was a mix of frustration and concern as he navigated the streets towards the station. "I hope you realize how serious this is," he said, his eyes meeting mine in the rearview mirror. "Sneaking around at night, getting caught by an armed homeowner... It's not just about breaking a promise, or being too nosy. It's about safety. You're lucky that Chad only called me. He very well could have shot you both."

We were well and truly chagrined as the cruiser pulled into the station's parking lot, both Cassie and I quiet and ready to run away with our tail between our legs. Ryan parked with a thoughtful frown. "Let's go inside. I need to hear everything, and I mean everything, about this."

Inside the station, Ryan and Ty ushered us into an interrogation room, and Cocoa followed. Ryan took the vial from me and left us alone with Ty for a minute. I was happy to see that the dog had enough smarts to sit on *our* side of the table, perpetrator that he was. The seriousness of the situation hung in the air, but there was a glimmer of something else too—maybe it was hope.

When Ryan came back, Cassie and I ran through our reasons for exploring Brenda's backyard and I am happy to say that we did not flinch or cower, despite the mens' stony expressions. We explained every detail, from the moment we decided to investigate to finding the vial. Ryan listened intently, his expression growing increasingly contemplative.

When we finished, he leaned back in his chair, rubbing his chin. "If this vial is what you think it is, it would change everything. But I have to be clear with both of you—this doesn't excuse what you did."

"We understand," I said, meeting his gaze. "But we had to act. We couldn't just sit back and do nothing. My business is on the line."

Ryan stood up, a sigh escaping him. "Please go home now and stay there until we hear back about the vial. I don't want to have to arrest you two, but I will do it if you push me. This is serious business. Who knows what Chad Larson is capable of if he really did kill Weiss. I want you to stay quiet and stay safe. Promise me?"

Cassie and I looked at each other and didn't even cross our

fingers behind our backs. "We promise." I was bone-dead tired and sick to death of sleuthing. Besides, I had a bed waiting for me after we got back home. I wasn't planning on going anywhere for a while.

"Good." Ryan opened the door. "You're free to go. But remember, I'm holding you to that promise."

As we left the station with Ty, who was going to drive us over to the Weiss neighborhood to pick up Cassie's truck, the weight of the night's events settled over me. From the successful party I'd catered to the questionable sleuthing and possible major evidence we'd found, it had been a wild ride. If I was being honest, I was surprised I'd made it through the day without collapsing, mentally or physically.

The only thing I could think about as we headed back home in Cassie's truck with Cocoa a few minutes later, was getting some shut-eye.

# Chapter Thirty-One

Sunday morning dawned with a calm that felt almost surreal after the chaos of the previous night. Cassie and I lounged on the sofa with our coffee, each lost in our thoughts. Cocoa, sensing our subdued mood, nuzzled against us in quiet companionship.

It had been one heck of a twenty-four hours and I knew that it would take me a while to recover from everything we'd been through. I still wasn't sure where I stood with Ryan after everything that had happened between us. I wasn't sure if I'd forgiven him for what happened at Weiss's funeral and I wasn't sure if he would forgive me for what we'd done the night before.

I checked my phone relentlessly, regardless, hoping to hear something from him, either about the mystery and the vial or the personal drama between us. But nothing came.

"Maybe we should go get some donuts," Cassie suggested, breaking the long silence that surrounded us.

I shrugged. "I guess." The truth was, I didn't feel much like eating. My emotions were all jumbled up, and it was messing with my stomach. Not a good sign at all.

Cocoa's ears perked up suddenly just before the doorbell rang. I frowned at Cassie and she frowned back.

"Were you expecting someone?" I asked.

She shook her head and hopped up to answer the door, Cocoa fast on her heels. I stood up too and glanced down at myself, wishing I wasn't still in my pjs. At least they were a cute matching set, rather than the usual mismatch I sported when sleeping.

Patty Larson stood on the step and Cocoa bounced around to say hi. She smiled down at him and then turned her smile to Cassie.

"Hi, I'm Patty. I was wondering if I could talk to Abby for a minute?"

I came up behind Cassie and gave Patty a smile. "Good morning! Come on in."

She followed me inside and Cassie shut the door.

"I don't want to take up too much of your time. I just wanted to come by and warn you about my husband." Her face clouded over, and I shot Cassie a worried look.

I motioned to the couch, but she shook her head. "I can't stay. He might have followed me. I just wanted to let y'all know that he knows it was you digging in our yard last night. You aren't safe."

Blushing, I made a face. "Sorry about that. It was technically this little guy," I said and pointed to Cocoa. "We weren't planning on going into your yard at all."

She waved my apology away. "It doesn't matter. The point is, he knows it was you in the yard and that you found something. He's probably gonna come after you."

There were tears in her eyes and she wiped them quickly away. "I knew something was up when he wanted to come to the festival with me. He never goes to those kinds of things."

She began to pace, and I crossed my arms over my chest, my mind racing. "Actually, it was even before that. It began when that lobbyist showed up and started talking to him. They met one day after he had visited Andy Weiss. Chad happened to be out in the yard that day and they got to talking about Weiss. About how Chad hated him. Then they met a few other times. Every time, Chad seemed more and more angry with the neighbors. I knew that man was spinning Chad up, making him crazy. And then Chad came with me to the festival and that's when Andy died." Tears spilled down her cheeks, then and her voice pitched. "Died from eating *my* food. My delicious food that I worked so hard on. That Chad poisoned."

At that moment, Chad Larson burst through the door, pointing a gun at us all. Cocoa yipped and ran at him quick as lightning, but Chad kicked him to the side without a second thought. With a whimper, Cocoa crumpled in the corner and my heart burst apart. The only thing keeping me from running to our little guy and scooping him into my arms was the gun pointed in my face.

"Stay where you are, you two busybodies. Patty, you need to come with me."

"I'm not going anywhere with you, Chad. I'm leaving you. I can't believe what a monster you've become. And for what? The stupid fence?"

He growled, and she flinched but held firm next to us. Out of the corner of my eye, I saw Cassie slowly pull her phone from her shorts pocket and start to type. I said a silent prayer that the lunatic with a gun wouldn't notice.

Patty Larson seemed to notice, though. She sighed and looked out the window, stalling him. "Why do you want to do this, honey? Isn't all the rest of it bad enough?"

"You can't leave. I can't let you leave me. We had plans. We are meant to be together. You promised you'd stick by me through thick and thin."

"Yeah, well, that was before you killed someone."

His face turned dark, and he eyed Cassie and I. Luckily, by then she'd slipped her phone back into her pocket.

"Stop it, Patty!" he yelled. "Don't say another word!"

"It's true, though. You killed the neighbor! And then you tried to kill Roblais at the funeral."

His nostrils flared, and he waved the gun wildly between the three of us. I glanced at Cocoa and sighed with relief when I saw his little eyes darting around. But his leg looked like it was at a wrong angle.

"It's too late Chad. The police have the vial. They know all about you," I said as calmly as I could, praying that Ryan would get here quick. It probably wasn't the smartest thing to say, given the man had a gun pointed at me and a wild look in his eye. But something in me broke, and I didn't care anymore. I glanced at Cocoa, lying in the corner. "They know what you did. It's only a matter of time before they find you and arrest you."

Chad growled and pointed the gun at me. My heart raced as I watched him debating whether to shoot me. I'd never felt so close to death.

"Patty, I'm warning you. If you say another word, I'll kill you all and be done with it! Now, come on. We gotta get out of here!"

Just then, Ryan and Ty burst through the door behind Chad, guns drawn. At the same time, Cocoa bounced up from the corner and dove at the man's ankle. He sunk his razor teeth into Chad's flesh and the man howled in pain. Before he could kick Cocoa a second time, Ryan and Ty had tackled him to the floor and grabbed the gun away from him, then slapped handcuffs onto his wrists.

Patty, Cassie, and I all cried as we watched, the pain and fear and absolute absurdity of what was happening flooding us with emotion. Cassie and I hugged Patty. She'd been through plenty, and no doubt, the road ahead would not be an easy one for her.

Ryan and Ty pulled Chad up off the ground and then Ty pushed him out the door with more force than I'd ever seen him use. The anger in his eyes was a shock. He'd always seemed like such a gentle, caring person. But I knew that he loved Cassie and he must be reeling at seeing her so close to harm.

Cocoa came over limping and I picked him up and hugged him to my chest. He'd been a true hero and I couldn't imagine my life without him. "You're such a good dog," I told him and he licked my face. Cassie moved to me too, tears in her eyes, and hugged us both. "Poor Cocoa Puff. What a good boy. What a brave boy."

Ryan watched us for a minute, breathing heavily with the adrenaline coursing through his body. His eyes gave away his emotions and my heart ached for putting him through so much stress and worry. He turned to Patty. "Ma'am, I know you've been through a lot. But would you mind coming with me and giving us a statement?"

She nodded, and I hugged her again. "It's going to be okay. Thank you so much for coming to warn us. That was a brave thing to do. Let's stay in touch."

With a small, sad smile, she nodded once more and then followed Ryan out the door.

Cassie and I stared at each other a moment after they left, both of us in absolute shock. But then Cocoa wriggled in my arms, bringing me back to the present.

"Let's get this little hero to the vet, pronto," I told her.

She nodded and grabbed her keys.

# Chapter Thirty-Two

After an agonizing wait at the vet, Cassie and I were relieved to find that Cocoa only had a broken leg. We'd been worried about internal injuries because of how hard Chad Larson had kicked him, but the vet assured us he'd be right as rain after the break healed. She set his leg and splinted it, then gave him the cone of shame, which did not suit his personality one bit. To his great disappointment, Cassie and I did not budge on his need to wear it, though, and so now he mostly sulked in his bed and glared at us, his characteristic bouncy energy all but zapped. We had no doubt it would return with gusto as soon as he was free of the ugly fashion piece, however.

By midweek, Cassie and I had finally mostly recovered from the craziness that had taken place over the last couple of weeks. She was back to focusing on antiquing rather than sleuthing, and I was trying my hardest to keep up with my business chores.

Unbeknownst to me, a food critic for a popular Fredericksburg publication had attended the dinner party at Aunt Meg's house the Saturday before, and had some glowing things to say about my food. I was already starting to get calls asking for my price list and was hard at work putting together literature and looking into a shiny website for Deep in the Heart Catering. There was much to do, but the attention energized me. Aunt Meg was already seeing an increase in reservations as well, and I hoped it had to do with being mentioned in the article.

Cassie waited for popcorn to finish in the microwave and smiled as she glanced over at me on the couch. "You're reading that review again, aren't you?"

I blushed and grinned. "I can't help it!" I scanned the article and read out loud. "Deep in the Heart Catering has undoubtedly raised the bar for culinary excellence in Sugar Creek. Abby Hirsch has not only showcased her remarkable skills as a chef but also her ability to create an atmosphere where food becomes the medium of connection and joy." It wasn't the New York Times food section or anything, but it was glowing and it felt darn good. I would take it any day of the week.

Cassie laughed. "It's good press, no doubt about it. Finally, things are looking up. You deserve it, lady. You've worked really hard and been through some seriously rough setbacks."

She moved to the couch with a big bowl of popcorn and plopped down next to Cocoa, who perked up at the smell of food.

"It's been crazy, that's no lie," I replied and stuffed a handful of buttery crunch into my mouth. Just then, there was a knock at the door. I frowned at Cassie, my mouth half full.

Cassie got a mischievous smile, and I frowned even more. "Who is it, Cassie?" I asked her with a glare. I knew that smirk, and I didn't like what she was up to.

She held onto Cocoa so he couldn't jump down and hurt his healing leg, and motioned to the door. "Go see!"

I hesitated and finished chewing, then fluffed my hair and wished I would have chosen something a little cuter to wear than old cutoff shorts and a t-shirt that said "Grilling Season."

Sure enough, Ryan and Ty stood on the other side, waiting

there with grins and a six-pack of local beer. "Hey, Abby," Ty said as he moved inside to plant a kiss on Cassie's cheek. Ryan stood on the step and we gazed at each other for a long minute. He wore shorts and a t-shirt as well which made me feel a little better about my attire. The dimpled grin he gave me as we stared at each other sent chills up my spine.

"Can I come in?" he asked and then craned his neck to glance at Cocoa on the couch. "Or am I still in the doghouse?" He laughed and my heart fluttered.

"Come on in," I told him.

As he passed, he grabbed my hand and squeezed. "It's good to see you," he said. "You look good."

It was probably a lie, but I would take it. Ty and Cassie were in the kitchen, sipping beer out of glasses and I followed Ryan in and shut the door, putting a hand to my flushed cheek.

Cassie poured Ryan and I beers as well and then held up her glass. "Well, y'all, here's to another successful murder investigation, and to clearing Abby's name!"

The men smiled and held their glasses up and I did too, happy that neither of them grumbled or made any comments about non-sanctioned sleuthing.

"And here's to Sugar Creek's very own amateur sleuthing duo, who somehow once again got the drop on us professionals," Ryan said and winked at me, then laughed. Cocoa harrumphed over in his bed and put his coned head on his paws. Clearly he thought he should get some recognition too. "And to the dog who saved them!" Ty finished, holding his beer in a salute to our little dog.

We all took another drink and then Ryan's face grew serious. "I thought you ladies would like to know what happened with Chad and Roblais."

"Of course we would!" Cassie said. She motioned us to the dining table, and we all sat.

"It took a while to get the whole story, and Patty Larson was a big help with filling in the blanks," Ryan began. "But after we talked to Chad Larson a while he finally opened up and told us that Roblais had been egging him on to kill Weiss. And once he finally *did* kill him, Roblais tried to hold that knowledge over his head in order to get him to run for city council in Mr. Weiss's place and vote for his bill. Chad got so angry about being blackmailed that he decided to do away with Roblais too. But Roblais was a lot bigger than Andy and he never finished his drink, so it didn't have the intended effect."

"So I guess in the end, it really was about the bill. But not in the way we all thought," I said and grabbed another handful of popcorn from the bowl Cassie had placed in the center of the table.

We talked a while longer and then decided to fire up an old movie. Cassie and Ty settled in on the couch and I suddenly got uncomfortable. I glanced at Cocoa, who seemed fidgety to me.

"I think I'll take Cocoa out for a quick potty break," I told them and grabbed his leash. He wasn't able to do a lot of walking, but he could at least get up from time to time to do his business. Now seemed as good a time as any.

"Mind if I come with you?" Ryan asked.

I turned to gaze at him, his blue eyes earnest, his mouth quirked.

"Sure," I said as I clipped the leash to Cocoa's collar.

The night was beautifully clear, and the heat had finally settled to a balmy 90. We strolled slowly behind the dog as he sniffed the grass, both of us quiet. I wasn't totally sure how I felt about him still, but it seemed silly to be mad at someone who saved my life only a few days before.

"I thought you agreed to have dinner at my place," he said after a few minutes, breaking the silence.

"Well, that was before you arrested me."

"I didn't arrest you, honey. I questioned you."

I rolled my eyes, but then I smiled, suddenly ready to put it all behind me and start again with this sweet beautiful man. "I'm game, if you are. Just tell me when."

He grabbed my arm and pulled me back into him. Our bodies pressed against each other and a shiver ran from the tips of my toes to the roots of my hair as he leaned in and gave me a wildly passionate kiss. Cocoa barked at us, unhappy to have his walk hijacked, but we paid him no mind. After a long embrace, we finally let go of each other and both of us were grinning from ear to ear.

"I need more of that in my life," Ryan told me as he grabbed my hand.

As we angled Cocoa back toward Cassie's cottage I leaned into him. "Me, too."

---

Thank you so much for reading Death and Peaches, book two of the Sugar Creek Mystery Series! I hope you enjoyed it!

Can't wait to get back to Sugar Creek with Abby and the gang? Death and Fondue, book three in the Sugar Creek Mystery Series is available for preorder now!

Preorder Book 3: Death and Fondue Now!

**A picturesque Texas vineyard. A tech company retreat turned deadly. A caterer caught in a bubbling pot of mystery.**

Abby Hirsch has established herself as the go-to caterer in her beloved hometown of Sugar Creek, Texas. But her skills are put to the test when a high-profile tech company from California chooses her aunt's charming bed and breakfast for their corporate retreat. Abby's ready to showcase her culinary talents, until the event turns sour with the mysterious death of the company's CEO, Barry Golding.

As the CEO's past misdeeds come to light and tensions within the tech group rise, Abby finds herself caught in a melting pot of secrets and egos. The vineyard setting is ripe with secrets, and everyone has a motive for murder. With the retreat descending into chaos and her reputation on the line, Abby must navigate through the tangled web of corporate intrigue and personal vendettas.

As things heat up both in the kitchen and with Sheriff Ryan Iverson, Abby slices through layers of intrigue to uncover the truth with the help of her best friend Cassie and their furry companion Cocoa. But can she dip into her sleuthing skills to serve justice before the killer strikes again?

Buy Book 3: Death and Fondue Now!

*Read on for the first chapter of Death and Fondue!*

---

*Want more cozy fun in your inbox?*

I send out a newsletter twice a month with personal stories, giveaways, recipes, polls, reading recommendations, and other fun surprises – along with the latest updates on my books!

I'd love to stay connected with you. Follow the link below to subscribe.

Subscribe To Nova's Newsletter
https://novawalsh.com/novas-newsletter/

# Peach and Goat Cheese Tart

**INGREDIENTS**

1 sheet puff pastry, thawed
2 ripe peaches, thinly sliced
8 oz goat cheese, softened
1 Tbsp cream or half & half
1 Tbsp honey
1 tsp fresh thyme leaves or 1/2 tsp dried thyme
Salt and pepper to taste
Mint for garnishing (if desired)

**DIRECTIONS**

1. Preheat your oven to 375°F.

2. Roll out the puff pastry on a floured surface and transfer to a baking sheet lined with parchment paper.

3. Mix the goat cheese, thyme, cream or half & half, salt and pepper together and spread evenly over the pastry, leaving a small border around the edges.

4. Arrange the peach slices on top of the goat cheese in an overlapping pattern.

5. Drizzle honey over the peaches and sprinkle with salt, pepper, and thyme leaves.

6. Bake for 25-30 minutes or until the pastry is golden and puffy.

7. Garnish with chopped mint and more honey if desired.

# Chicken and Peach Skewers

**INGREDIENTS**

For the Skewers:

1½ pounds chicken thighs, boneless and skinless, cut into chunks

3 ripe peaches, cut into wedges

1 large red onion, cut into chunks

Salt and pepper to taste

Olive oil, for drizzling

For the Marinade:

¼ cup olive oil

¼ cup peach juice (freshly squeezed from ripe peaches or store-bought)

2 tablespoons honey

2 cloves garlic, minced

1 teaspoon fresh or dried thyme leaves

Salt and pepper to taste

**DIRECTIONS**

• In a large bowl, whisk together olive oil, peach juice, honey, garlic, thyme, rosemary, salt, and pepper.

• Add the chicken chunks to the marinade, ensuring they are well coated. Cover and refrigerate for at least 1 hour, or up to 4 hours for more flavor.

• If using wooden skewers, soak them in water for at least 30 minutes to prevent burning.

• Thread the marinated chicken, peach wedges, and red onion chunks alternately onto the skewers.

• Preheat the grill to medium-high heat. Drizzle the skewers with a little olive oil and season with salt and pepper.

• Grill the skewers, turning occasionally, until the chicken is thoroughly cooked and the peaches and onions are slightly charred, about 10-15 minutes.

• Serve the skewers hot, garnished with fresh thyme or rosemary if desired.

# Summer Panzanella Salad

**INGREDIENTS**

4 cups rustic bread, cut into 1-inch cubes (preferably day-old, for better texture)

2 tablespoons olive oil

2 cups ripe tomatoes, chopped into bite-sized pieces

1 cup cucumber, sliced

1/2 cup red onion, thinly sliced

1/2 cup fresh basil leaves, torn

1/4 cup fresh mozzarella

For the dressing:

1/3 cup extra-virgin olive oil

3 tablespoons balsamic vinegar

1 garlic clove, minced

Salt and freshly ground black pepper, to taste

**DIRECTIONS**

- Preheat the oven to 375°F
- Toss the bread cubes with 2 tablespoons of olive oil
- Spread the bread cubes on a baking sheet in a single layer.

• Bake for 10-15 minutes, or until the bread is toasted and golden brown. Let cool.

• In a small bowl, whisk together the extra-virgin olive oil, balsamic vinegar, minced garlic, salt, and pepper until well combined.

• In a large bowl, combine the toasted bread, tomatoes, cucumber, red onion, basil leaves, and mozzarella.

• Drizzle the dressing over the salad and toss gently to combine. Let the salad sit for about 10-30 minutes before serving, allowing the bread to absorb the dressing and flavors to meld.

# Death and Fondue
# Chapter One

*Texas is a state of mind.*

Truer words were never spoken, if you ask me. Leave it to John Steinbeck to say things eloquently. His quote bounced around my head as I watched the latest gaggle of visitors descend on my Aunt Meg's B&B, Primrose House, midmorning on the first Thursday of August. The group of them bustled in through the front door with roller bags and clicking heels and a seriousness I hadn't experienced since I'd left L.A. back in June.

I'd been at the B&B since early morning, knocking out a load of prep work for a golden anniversary party I was catering the following day which is why I was able to observe the group of tech entrepreneurs firsthand as they landed in Aunt Meg's quaint and cozy farmhouse. The dissonance between Texas cordial and California cool was jarring, to say the least.

"Hey, Barry, check this out," one man said as the group set their laptop bags and purses down on the furniture in the lobby area. He wore a black turtleneck and jeans despite the summer heat. I doubted the getup would last him very long. He'd be in a t-shirt by Saturday. He pointed to a landscape painting of rolling hills of bluebonnets and cattle grazing that hung above the fireplace and guffawed.

"Talk about Podunk. Is this place for real?"

I rolled my eyes as I continued to watch them. The watercolor was one of a limited set from a talented local artist who'd recently had his own retrospective collection in the Modern Art Museum in Fort Worth.

The other man, who must have been Barry, raised an eyebrow and then turned back to his phone without acknowledging the comment. He had thick gray hair and wore designer jeans and an untucked button-down shirt. As well as the most ugly lime green high-tops I'd ever seen, the kind that looked straight out of an 80s movie.

I set out a tray of monster cookies I'd baked that morning, peanut butter and oatmeal mounds bursting with decadent chocolate chunks and dried cherries, and adjusted the tray so it caught the light in an enticing way. Looking up, one woman—the one with platinum blonde hair cut in a fierce bob and wearing a serious navy suit—glanced at the cookies with a scowl.

"Those must be a thousand calories apiece," she mumbled without looking at me, and then she too turned back to her phone.

I reserved my second eye roll and my snarky comments for when I was back in the kitchen by myself. The guest is always right, after all.

The man who'd commented on the painting plopped down onto the lovely blue sofa that sat in the front window next to another much younger man who had thick brown shaggy hair and they both pulled laptops out of their bags. "Hey, what's the Wi-Fi password?" the younger one shouted out to the room. I grabbed one of the printed welcome sheets Aunt Meg had on the check-in desk in the corner and handed it to him. He took it wordlessly without looking at me.

The second woman of the group approached the check-in desk

as she pulled a sheaf of papers out of her own laptop bag. She looked to be younger than the rest of them, had long dark brown hair, and was dressed in slim designer jeans and bright red heels so high I couldn't imagine how she got around all day. Those things would have killed my back.

"Are you Margaret? I'm Cheryl, from NexTech Dynamics. I emailed you about our reservation?" Her voice was brisk, but there was an underlying note of fatigue. "I have our itinerary here, and a list of dietary preferences and... um, special requests from the group."

Aunt Meg raised her eyebrows and took the papers the woman handed her without looking at them. "Hi Cheryl. I'm Meg. I own Primrose House. We have everything prepared for your stay. Don't you worry about a thing."

The woman gazed around nervously and bit her lip. "It's very important that these requests are met in a timely manner. We are in the middle of a very important decision-making process for our company right now and our people need everything to be exactly right so they can focus on the job at hand. If you cannot accommodate these requests, we'll have to find a place elsewhere..."

Aunt Meg cut her off with a friendly smile. "No, of course. I understand and I'll make sure every item is taken care of if it's in our power to do so. It looks like you've booked five rooms with us for the week. And I see you reserved a suite for a Barry Golding?" Aunt Meg looked over her glasses to the room and the man in the ugly high-tops stuck his hand up without looking up from his phone.

Aunt Meg looked from him to Cheryl, trying to decide who she should be addressing.

"I'll be taking care of everything for the group, so if you could just give me the keys and let me know where to find the rooms, I'll figure it out. Thanks."

Aunt Meg's part-time helper, Maria, came in just then and Aunt Meg motioned her over. "This is Maria," she told the woman. "She's wonderful, and will help you with anything you need during your stay. Maria, do you mind showing our guests to their rooms?"

Maria smiled her warm smile and took the group of keys. "If you'll all follow me," she said and waited for the group to collect their things and follow her up the stairs.

"Yo, Eric, your room's ready, man," the turtlenecked one said to the guy still hacking away on his laptop on the couch. He let out a sharp whistle, and I flinched.

The man on the couch, Eric, stood up, his laptop still open and balanced in one hand as he grabbed his stuff and followed the group up the stairs, still staring at the laptop. I hoped he wouldn't fall. The last thing we needed was for one of them to die.

"Woo! You've got your work cut out for you," I told Aunt Meg as I paced the front room.

She frowned as she looked over the sheaf of papers Cheryl had given her. I moved to her side to peer over her shoulder at the strange requests the group had made.

- *NO PEANUTS, SEVERE ALLERGY*
- *on-call theta energy healer*
- *spirulina and acai for morning smoothies*
- *bulletproof coffee*
- *eco friendly organic cleaning products used for all the rooms*
- *conference space with dedicated Wi-Fi*

"Bless their hearts," Aunt Meg said, and we both burst out laughing.

Not that we didn't take their requests seriously, or that we didn't respect every guest that came to stay at Primrose House. We were grateful for their business and would absolutely try to make them comfortable and treat them with hospitality and kindness, like every guest who came through the front door of the B&B. But there are just some things that are not immediately available in a small town in Texas. Like an energy healer, for instance. At least not that I knew of, although times had changed in our little corner of the world, just like everywhere else.

"Good thing they acted like the monster cookies were poison... because to at least one of them they would be." Monster cookies were chock full of peanut butter. I swiftly removed the tray of them from the sideboard. I'd take them home to Cassie, or drop them by the station on my way home. It would give me an excuse to see Ryan Iverson, the sheriff who I was sort of seeing at present, although we hadn't really defined our relationship yet.

"The conference room, at least, won't be a problem," Aunt Meg said. She'd turned the old formal dining room into a meeting area just recently as she'd begun getting more business groups staying at the B&B thanks to a campaign we were running with the Sugar Creek chamber of commerce. It was only one of several new marketing efforts to pump some energy into Aunt Meg's struggling business. Another of them was adding dinner parties and other events, catered by my brand new company, Deep in the Heart Catering.

She nodded. "I guess I could ask around about the healer thing. Georgie might know," Aunt Meg said as she frowned and pulled up the internet. "Or maybe I'll just Google it."

I patted her on the back, not at all envious of the tasks she was about to take on. "I'll get some new cleaning supplies when I stop by the store this afternoon and see what I can do about the food. There are a few more things I have to get for this anniversary party, anyway. If I can't find anything, I guess we could order it to be delivered. Might not get here right away, but we'll do our best, right? And if they have a problem with that, then we will wish them luck and send them on their way. It's okay, Aunt Meg. They probably won't even notice whether half of that stuff is here."

She looked worried despite my reassurance, but nodded as she dived into her search for alternative healers in the hill country. I knew she took her job very seriously and wouldn't rest until every guest was satisfied, no matter how crazy their demands were. Her drive to please every guest was why her B&B had such a great reputation.

Heading back to the kitchen, I thought about what else I needed to get done for the anniversary party I was catering before the end of the day. I'd made three layers of round decadent fudge cakes earlier and they were cooling on wire racks on the sideboard. I would mix up the cherry filling and chocolate icing a little later. Tomorrow, I would fill and ice the cake right before the party.

The menu for the event was simple, but satisfying. Pulled pork with brown sugar caramelized onions, freshly made sweet rolls and cucumber pickles, German potato salad with thin-sliced red onion and capers in a tangy vinaigrette, a Brussels sprout slaw, and garlic green beans for the main event, plus plenty of snacks and tidbits to keep the fifty person guest list grazing for as long as the party went on. I took a few moments to gather lemon, dill, chives, vinegar, and oil for the dressing I would use for the potato salad, and then chopped through the fragrant herbs.

I'd met the Lancaster family two weeks before, when Maddie Lancaster had called to set the party up for her parents. I was overjoyed to help with the fifty-year anniversary party for fifty people that would take place in the Lancaster backyard—the same place they'd been married so many years before. It was the still the height of summer, so it would likely be a warm night. We'd decided on a buffet set up inside the house for guests to come and go as they wished. I wouldn't be servicing this time around, but doing setup and takedown only. I was sad I wouldn't get to see the party in full swing because I always loved to see people enjoying my food, but a job was a job and I was happy for the work.

Since I'd moved back in June, Deep in the Heart Catering had been slowly but steadily growing. A few people in town were still under the mistaken impression that I'd poisoned someone because of an unfortunate funeral I'd catered when I'd first returned to town, but most of the locals had come around quickly and a few nicely worded reviews had helped to get things rolling. I wasn't as busy as I wanted to be, but I was busy enough to keep my little business going, and that was the main thing. It would take time, but if I stuck with it, this catering business of mine would grow and eventually thrive. I was certain of it.

Maria came in as I was mixing up the lemon dill vinaigrette for the potato salad.

"Did you get the group squared away?" I asked her as I poured oil in a steady stream with one hand and whisked furiously with the other.

A small smile played on her lips. "Hopefully. They are certainly a needy bunch. They asked for pure ionized mineral water. Do you know if that's what this is?" she asked as she held one of the little plastic bottles we stored in a drink fridge for guests up in the air.

I frowned. "Probably not."

Maria frowned back and folded her arms. "I guess I should go to the store."

I finished with the vinaigrette and used a funnel to pour it into a dressing container so I could easily use it the next day. "No, it's okay. I'm heading over there now, anyway, and I can get water and the other stuff on their list. I'll try, at least."

Maria smiled. "Thank you, I appreciate it. I don't know why it matters, exactly what kind of water we have. You would think that bottled water would be good enough. Even tap water here is good enough for me."

I raised my eyebrows and cleaned up the kitchen quickly, then hung my apron on a hook in the pantry. "I don't know. It could be they're testing us. Or maybe they really believe there's something bad in the other water. Who knows? Doesn't matter. Like Aunt Meg says, the guest comes first. I shouldn't take too long, I only have a few things to buy for the party tomorrow. Call me if they ask for anything else while I'm gone."

As I grabbed my keys and purse and headed out the kitchen door with my trusty notebook, I was assaulted with a wave of air so hot it felt like I'd stepped into an oven. Good old Texas summer, there was nothing quite like it. Too bad there was so much of it. August was always the worst. It was right in the middle of the heat. You'd already gotten your fill and yet you knew there were still a couple more months to endure before it would even hint at cooling off. I pushed my sweaty hair off my face as I headed toward my car in the gravel parking lot in the front of the B&B.

It would be a long few days with the California people. I could feel the storm coming. At least I didn't have to cater to their every whim. My only official catering job for them would be a group dinner they had planned at Wild Hare Winery for Saturday night. I sat a moment as the air conditioning in my car struggled to life and made a couple of notes to myself about meeting with Cheryl later to hammer out the details for the event. I'd only gotten a brief idea of what they'd had in mind for their dinner when they'd booked the reservation, and I needed to cement it all down with her when I returned.

But one problem at a time, I told myself as I backed out of the parking lot and turned toward downtown Sugar Creek.

One problem at a time.

---

# Also by Nova Walsh

## The Sugar Creek Mystery Series

*Love cozy mysteries with a side of delicious treats? Check out my Sugar Creek Mystery Series, where small-town sleuths solve crimes and whip up culinary delights!*

Death and Wedding Cake

Death and Peaches

Death and Fondue

Death and Blackberry Pie

Death and Eggnog

Death and Groom's Cake (Coming February 2025)

Christmas in Sugar Creek (Short Story Collection)

## The Moonstone Bakery Mystery Series

Lava Cake and Lies

Cupcakes and Crime (Coming March 2025)

## The Maple Grove Romance Series

The Cozy Corner Book Store

The Sugar Stop Chocolate Shop

# About Nova Walsh

Author Nova Walsh writes culinary cozy mysteries full of humor, shenanigans, and friendships that last a lifetime. She mixes in a healthy dose of amateur sleuthing, some slow-burn romance, and a pinch of comedy in every book she writes.

Nova is a former chef/caterer who still loves to cook but loves to write even more. She's an enthusiastic, if not totally successful gardener and loves travel, wine, and hanging out with friends.

Nova lives in central Texas with her husband, son, and two delightfully crazy pups. When she isn't writing, she's often cooking, gardening, hiking, or reading a good book with a pup by her side.

You can contact Nova at nova@novawalsh.com

www.ingramcontent.com/pod-product-compliance
Lightning Source LLC
LaVergne TN
LVHW010058170826
845678LV00012B/2164

*9798224896103*